Not I,
Said the Sparrow

MYSTERIES BY RICHARD LOCKRIDGE

Not I, Said the Sparrow
Write Murder Down
Something Up a Sleeve
Death in a Sunny Place
Inspector's Holiday
Preach No More
Twice Retired
Troubled Journey

A Risky Way to Kill
Die Laughing
A Plate of Red Herrings
Murder in False-Face
With Option to Die
Murder for Art's Sake
Squire of Death
Murder Can't Wait

Murder Roundabout

OTHER BOOKS BY RICHARD LOCKRIDGE

One Lady, Two Cats
A Matter of Taste

The Empty Day
Encounter in Key West

Mr. and Mrs. North

BOOKS BY FRANCES AND RICHARD LOCKRIDGE
MR. AND MRS. NORTH

Murder by the Book
Murder Has Its Points
The Judge Is Reversed
Murder Is Suggested
The Long Skeleton
Voyage into Violence
Death of an Angel
A Key to Death
Death Has a Small Voice
Curtain for a Jester
Dead as a Dinosaur
Murder Comes First
The Dishonest Murderer

Murder Is Served
Untidy Murder
Death of a Tall Man
Murder Within Murder
Payoff for the Banker
Killing the Goose
Death Takes a Bow
Hanged for a Sheep
Death on the Aisle
Murder Out of Turn
A Pinch of Poison
The Norths Meet Murder
Murder in a Hurry

CAPTAIN HEIMRICH

The Distant Clue
First Come, First Kill
With One Stone
Show Red for Danger
Accent on Murder
Practise to Deceive
Let Dead Enough Alone
Burnt Offering

Death and the Gentle Bull
Stand Up and Die
Death by Association
A Client Is Canceled
Foggy, Foggy Death
Spin Your Web, Lady
I Want to Come Home
Think of Death

MYSTERY ADVENTURES

The Devious Ones
Quest of the Bogeyman
Night of Shadows
The Ticking Clock
And Left for Dead
The Drill Is Death

The Golden Man
Murder and Blueberry Pie
The Innocent House
Catch as Catch Can
The Tangled Cord
The Faceless Adversary

CATS

Cats and People

Not I, Said the Sparrow

An Inspector Heimrich mystery

by Richard Lockridge

J. B. LIPPINCOTT COMPANY
Philadelphia & New York

U.S. Library of Congress Cataloging in Publication Data

Lockridge, Richard, birth date
    Not I, said the sparrow.

    I. Title.
PZ3.L81144No [PS3523.0245]   813'.5'2   73–1818
ISBN–0–397–00962–3

For Hildy

1

By mid-September in the latitude of the town of Van
Brunt, Putnam County, State of New York, one begins
to snatch at mild sunny days, which soon will be in
short supply. Frost may come at any time; snow is not
as far away as it once was. Ice will cover the terrace of
a long, low house above the Hudson River. Tall bright
marigolds will become shriveled hulks of plants and
have to be dragged up by the roots. But it was sunny
and warm that Saturday, and Merton Heimrich was
having as near a day off as he ever gets, and they were
having prelunch drinks on the terrace.

It was a little after noon, and Heimrich, Inspector,
New York State Police, had just put a tray with two tall
drinks on it on a table when the mail carrier honked
twice from the foot of the steep driveway. Susan had
started to reach out toward her glass, but she drew her
hand back. There is a ritual.

"He's early today," Susan said.

Heimrich said, "Well, after all, it's Saturday," and walked down the steep driveway—a big man who walked with long, sure strides. Susan watched him and her lips formed into a smile. She thought, fleetingly, of hippopotamuses, to which Merton Heimrich sometimes, when in a low state of mind, compares himself. Her smile widened. She shook her head. There was a gentle breeze, and it ruffled her short brown hair a little.

Heimrich went over the hump in the driveway and disappeared between the two boulders on either side of it where it joins High Road. It was a quiet day, and she could hear the rasp of the mailbox's opening and of its snapping closed again. Her husband appeared over the driveway's hump, and his strides were as long and sure up the steep grade as they had been when he went down it. Hippopotamus indeed, Susan Heimrich thought.

He had one hand full. "Mostly junk," he said, as he spread the day's mail on the table beside the tray. "But a letter from the boy."

The boy is Michael Faye and Susan's son. He has grown tall since Heimrich first met him, which was when he was a small grave boy named after his father, who had died in Korea long before Heimrich looked for the first time at a slim, tall young woman with tiredness in her face and the lines of strain, and thought, She isn't really pretty, and why is it so pleasant, so almost exciting, to look at her?

There was no strain in her face that noon. They clicked tall glasses together and sipped from them, and Susan opened the letter, which was addressed to Inspector and Mrs. M. L. Heimrich. It was postmarked "Hanover, N.H." and must, Susan thought, have been mailed almost as soon as he had got back to Dartmouth for his junior year. I'm lucky in my son, Susan thought. Nowadays so many of them seem to turn entirely into somebody else. It's natural they should, she thought. But I'm glad he stays Michael. "Dear Mother and Dad," she read. I'm glad he doesn't call me "Mom" and that he never did. I'm glad he calls Merton "Dad" instead of "sir."

"There was frost last night," she read. "The leaves are turning. But the courts are still all right and I got Professor Arnold for Eng. Lit. III. And Frank and I got a room together and it's one of the ones with a bathroom. Believe it or not."

She read on while Merton shuffled through the mail, which was indeed mostly "junk." There were several appeals for contributions, largely for causes which most Van Bruntians would consider left wing. The Heimrichs are members of the NAACP. Mailing lists get passed around. They are also members of Common Cause. One thing leads to another.

"He's got his first service working again, he thinks," Susan said. "He's getting more top spin on his forehand." Young Michael, the spring before, had played in the number two spot on the Dartmouth tennis team. His first service had tended to go too deep. "He thinks he may get on the staff of the school paper. But I'll let you read it yourself. It's not very long."

"What's 'The Tor?'" Heimrich asked her.

"A steep rocky hill," Susan said. "Also part of the title of a play by Maxwell Anderson. He says he's got all the money he needs. For now. What's about a tor?"

"*The* Tor," Merton told her. "Here." He slid a square white envelope toward her. He slid it face down. On the flap the words "The Tor, Highlands, New York" were embossed. They rose up thickly from the heavy white paper.

"It looks like a wedding announcement," Merton said, and picked up Michael's letter. Michael's typing was exact. So, for that matter, was Michael's backhand. And young Michael's grave mind.

"The Jameson place," Susan said. "What it's always been called. Oh, when I was quite a small girl, 'King Arthur's Tor.' We didn't know what 'tor' meant. I thought it was a castle. In a way it is, almost. But you must know it, dear."

"Oh," Merton Heimrich said, "that Tor. Yes. Mr. Jameson has always been a law-abiding sort. No official contact. What has he to say to the villagers?"

Susan had been turning the square white envelope over in her hands. It was addressed, in script which had the feel of formality, to Inspector and Mrs. M. L. Heimrich. She opened it, with the care she felt it deserved. The message, in the same script on a thick white card with "The Tor" engraved at the top, was brief.

"Cocktails and buffet on the twenty-third of September from six o'clock. Black tie." "RSVP" was in the lower left-hand corner of the card.

She handed the invitation to Merton. He read it. He said, "Why us? Why black tie at six o'clock in the country?"

"They've always been on the formal side," Susan said. "Keeping-up-the-traditions sort of thing. I don't know why us, dear. Except—"

She broke off. He looked at her and waited. When she merely looked off toward the river which sparkled below them in the sunlight, he said, "You speak as if you knew them. Mr. and Mrs. Jameson?"

"Mr. and Miss," Susan said. "Brother and sister. I suppose because, to them, I'm still the Upton girl. They must be quite old by now. My father and Arthur Jameson knew each other when they were young, which probably was at about the same time. Went to the same parties, I suppose. Knew the same people."

10

"Wore the same black ties?"

Susan laughed briefly. She said she supposed so.

"Old families together," she said. "Carrying on the old traditions, I suppose. It was before the Uptons lost their money, dear. Before I married Michael, who was from the Flats. Whose parents and grandparents had lived in the Flats. Who didn't belong. It must have been—oh, a strange sort of world. Of society. An anachronism nowadays. Probably even when I was very young. I didn't see much of it when I got old enough to remember. And when father didn't have the right kind of money any more. And of course after I married a Faye."

"And now a Heimrich," Merton said. "Which brings us back where we started, doesn't it? Back to why us? Merely because you were born an Upton?"

"I don't know," Susan said. "Perhaps because you're an inspector, dear. Makes you a V.I.P., probably."

It was Merton Heimrich's turn to laugh briefly.

"Policemen aren't V.I.P.s," he said. "Not to old Hudson River families."

"To the offspring of one of them," Susan said. "Very. Also, you have a dinner jacket, darling. You look fine in a dinner jacket."

"The Jameson place is twenty miles or so above Cold Harbor," Heimrich said. "It will be time for the equinoctial storms."

He was told that he knew that was nonsense; that a week from today might be as much like summer as today.

"Do you want to go?"

She looked off again toward the wide, sparkling river. After a moment she nodded her head. She amplified that slightly.

"Sort of," Susan said. "It might be fun. If it wasn't, we wouldn't have to stay long."

11

"It sounds like rather an austere kind of fun," Merton told her. "Black tie at six in the evening. And of course there may be a big-time murder about then. One's a little overdue."

Inspector M. L. Heimrich is a specialist in murder occurring in the southern counties of New York and not in urban areas. When he made inspector, Susan had hoped that the new rank would mean he sat at a desk and told others—others like Lieutenant Charles Forniss —what to do. She had hoped his hours would be more or less from nine to five, with weekends free. It had not worked out as she hoped. Heimrich has found old habits hard to break. In Susan's rather guarded opinion, he hasn't made much effort to break them.

"Excluding murder?" Susan said. "And hurricanes?"

"All right," Merton said. " 'Inspector and Mrs. M. L. Heimrich are happy to accept your kind invitation to cocktails and buffet on Saturday, the twenty-third, if violent death or hurricanes do not intervene.' Shall I make us another round?"

"Do that," Susan said. "Then I thought an omelet. With sausages? And perhaps avocado, if it's ever ripened."

"Fine," Heimrich said, and went off with empty glasses.

When he moves, Susan thought, it's sometimes almost as if he were dancing.

2

It was still sunny on Saturday, the twenty-third of September. The sun was a week lower in the west; it was a little cooler. But it was a fine late afternoon when they drove north on NY 11F toward Highlands, New York, which consists of a post office and a grocery store, licensed for the sale of beer, and a purveyor licensed by the Alcoholic Beverage Control Commission of the State of New York. Heimrich wore a dinner jacket which fitted smoothly over his wide shoulders. Susan wore a red and black dress, which fitted smoothly everywhere and was made from a fabric of her own design. She had a soft white sweater over her shoulders, in case it was cold coming back. The Buick purred. Heimrich had turned off the police radio so that it did not chatter at them. If all hell broke loose somewhere, Troop K could call the car by telephone.

Heimrich said it ought to be along here somewhere

and slowed the car. He said, "Were you ever at The Tor as a child?"

"It was never a place for children," Susan said. "Once or twice, I think. Probably when I was ten or eleven. A long time ago. I suppose it was during King Arthur's first marriage. They had a son, I think. Older than I was. Almost grown up, actually. But I don't really remember, dear. A blur, really. I don't know why Mother and Dad took me there. Up there where those stone posts are, I think. Go slower, Merton."

Merton Heimrich went more slowly.

Two fieldstone pillars, topped with globes, were set on either side of the opening of a drive. A metal plaque was set into each of the pillars, and on each plaque were the words: "The Tor." He turned into the drive, which was of bound gravel and mounted steeply to a turn. The Buick's tires grated on the gravel.

"Do you remember anything about this King Arthur?" Heimrich asked, as the car crept up to the curve in the driveway. "Or was it too long ago?"

"Richard Cory, sort of," Susan said, to which, negotiating the sharp curve and approaching a second one, Heimrich said "Huh?"

" 'A gentleman from sole to crown,' " Susan quoted. " 'Clean favored, and imperially slim.' You know the poem."

"He went home and put a bullet through his head," Heimrich said. "Yes."

He went around the second curve. It was a little like driving through a tunnel. Tall evergreens lined the drive on either side. The drive still wound upward. A "tor" is a high, rocky promontory. Another car showed close behind Heimrich in his rearview mirror, then disappeared as he entered still another curve.

14

"I begin to remember," Susan said. "It's a very long driveway and always twisting. The house is at the very top. It's a fieldstone house, I think. Gray. I think it's gray. It was—I think it was frightening to a little girl. So big and so gray. But I don't really remember. I—"

She stopped because Merton had clamped the brakes on hard. He had clamped them because a very large dog —a Doberman, he thought—stood in the middle of the driveway and showed no sign of standing anywhere else.

"My God," Heimrich said, "the hound of the Baskervilles." He honked at the dog. The dog took seconds to think this over. Then he turned and went up the driveway at a trot. "A sentinel?" Susan said, and Heimrich said, "Or a guard," and let the Buick creep up the grade behind the trotting dog. He added that this must be a hell of a thing to keep plowed in the winter.

"Oh," Susan said, "probably there are plenty of serfs."

There was light ahead, shining through the trees. Heimrich guided the car around another curve, and this was the final curve. He crept out of the tunnel into a wide, roughly circular, graveled area, bright under the floodlights on the roof of a three-story house. It was a house built of gray fieldstone, as Susan had remembered it. A dozen cars were parked around the circle, symmetrically nosing in toward the lawn beyond the paved spread. Heimrich turned the Buick into the parking area and thought, It's going to be one of those damn big brawls, and a youth in a white jacket and dark trousers and, a little inconsequentially, tennis shoes said, "I'll park it for you, sir—oh, it's you, Inspector."

Heimrich stopped the car and said, "Evening, Teddy. You're quite a way from home, aren't you?" to Theodore Carnes, who lived in Van Brunt.

"Sometimes I help out when people have parties,"

15

Carnes said, and went around the Buick and opened the door on Susan's side. "Came up on the Honda."

"I don't doubt it," Heimrich said. He knew Teddy Carnes's Honda, by sound and sight. Now and then it very noisily traversed High Road. It often banged its way along Van Brunt Avenue, dodging alarmingly among cars.

"Go right along in, Inspector, Mrs. Heimrich," Teddy said. "I'll park her for you."

Susan came around the car and stood by her husband. Teddy Carnes got into the Buick, and another car, a Mercedes, pulled up behind the Buick and stopped.

"So it's you I've been trailing," Sam Jackson said, and went around the Mercedes and opened the door for his wife. Susan said "Hi" to Mary and Samuel Jackson, and Heimrich said "Evening" to both of them. Jackson was very tall beside his wife, who was a slender five feet beside her more-than-six-foot husband. Mary Jackson said, "Darlings!" as she was likely to say, and held out her hands to Susan.

Teddy came back from parking the Buick and said, "I'll park it for you, sir," to Jackson, who said, "Do that, Teddy."

The four of them walked toward the big gray house, from which light poured and, as they drew nearer, music.

"The old boy's really laying it on tonight," Sam Jackson said. "A real birthday party."

Heimrich, walking beside Jackson, said, "Is it? We didn't know."

"His seventy-third, I think it is," Jackson said. "Or seventy-second. First time he's thrown this kind of party for one of them, far's I know. Far's we've been invited, anyway. Not like him, actually."

"I've never met him," Heimrich said, as they went

16

up wide, easy, stone steps toward the wide, brightly lighted door of the big house. "Invitation pretty much came out of the blue for us. Susan's parents knew the Jamesons, apparently. She vaguely remembers being brought here as a child."

"The Upton girl," Jackson said. "The Uptons. The Van Brunts before Cornelia started killing people and you caught her at it, M.L.* The Jamesons. The Frashinghams."

"And the Jacksons," Heimrich said.

"Yes," Samuel Jackson said. "I suppose you'd have to count us in. My father and his father. An 'our crowd' sort of thing, I guess. Before my time. I'm Arthur's attorney. Why we're here, I suppose."

Susan and Mary had reached the wide door. A Negro in a white jacket opened it, bowing. He said, "Everybody's in the drawing room, ladies. Gentlemen. You go right along in."

They went into a large, square room which contained half a dozen carved and forbidding wooden chairs and a refectory table. On their right, double glass doors stood open, and music came through the doorway and the sound of voices. A hell of a lot of voices, Merton thought. He does not approve of large parties. He wished they had stayed at home with Colonel, the outsize Great Dane, and Mite, the all-black tomcat. He and Susan followed the Jacksons through the doorway.

Just inside the double doors, the Jacksons stopped to shake hands with a tall, lean man in a dinner jacket and, unexpectedly, a wing collar. The man had thick gray hair and a long tanned face and if he was their host he was seventy-three—or seventy-two—and didn't look it.

* Heimrich arrested Mrs. Cornelia Van Brunt for murder in *Burnt Offering*.

17

"Mary!" the gray-haired man said. "Sam! Glad you could make it. So glad."

Which, of course, settled that.

Arthur Jameson looked beyond the Jacksons. He said, "Susan! You must be Susan Upton. You haven't changed a bit. My word, you haven't."

"I must have been about ten or eleven when you saw me last. I'm sure I've changed a bit. This is—"

"Inspector," Jameson said. "Inspector *Heimrich*. Delighted you could come, sir. Help an old codger with his little celebration. Probably you know everybody here."

"Good of you to have us, Mr. Jameson," Heimrich said, and looked around the big room—an enormous room, actually. A rectangular room, with a bar at the far end of it; with a tremendous fireplace midway of one of the long walls. There was an ornamental screen in front of the fireplace. There were twenty or more people in the room. All the men wore dinner jackets and most of the women bright dresses, some of them long dresses. At first glance Heimrich did not see anybody he knew.

"Get yourselves drinks," Jameson told them. "Or Barnes here will get them. See what they want, Barnes."

Barnes was a thin dark man in a white jacket, who had more or less appeared out of nowhere. He said, "Yes, sir, Mr. Jameson." Heimrich rather expected him to end the sentence with another "Sir," but he didn't. A crack in the ritual?

Heimrich looked down the long room toward the bar and, finally, saw a familiar face. Harold, until he had retired a year or so before, had been the bartender at the Old Stone Inn.

"Scotch and soda," Sam Jackson said, and Mary said, "Could I have a daiquiri, please?" And Heimrich said,

"Look who's tending bar, dear," and took Susan's arm and guided her down the room, among the strangers—a good many of whom, he thought, looked like being contemporaries of their host—toward the familiar face. When they reached the bar, Harold said, "Inspector. Mrs. Heimrich. The usual for both of you?"

The words had a pleasant sound. Susan said. "Please, Harold," and then, "No. I think I'll have a gin and tonic." Heimrich merely nodded his head at Harold, and Harold mixed a gin and tonic and a dry martini. He twisted lemon peel over the martini.

In the few minutes they had been in the big drawing room, it had become almost crowded. At the open double doors Arthur Jameson still was greeting arriving guests. People Heimrich did not know were converging on the bar, smiling, polite and clearly thirsty. "We're blocking traffic," Susan said, and they edged away from the bar, holding their glasses carefully, saying, "Sorry. If we may?" and getting smiles and polite movements from people they did not know. They reached what was, moderately, a clearing.

It was occupied by a tall, white-haired woman in a long black dress. The white hair was somewhat scanty; the long, deeply tanned face was crisscrossed by tiny wrinkles. She had a needlessly long, strong nose. She looked, Merton Heimrich thought, as if she had been well baked. She looked as if she had spent many summer days on golf courses.

She was not alone in this momentary breathing space. On one side of her was a tall and substantial young man with blond hair cut short. His dinner jacket was dark blue and his "black" tie matched it. He had a wide smile which appeared to have been grafted onto his face. Bored politeness fixes smiles in place.

On the other side of the woman in black was a startlingly pretty young woman—a slim young woman in a sleeveless white dress. She had blue eyes of surprising size and blond hair which drifted in waves to her shoulders. Her smile, too, looked fixed in place. But so, Heimrich thought, must ours. He also thought, hopefully, that there must be chairs somewhere. Somewhere, preferably, in a corner. They had almost smiled past the three when the white-haired woman said, "You must be Susan Upton." She spoke firmly, in a low, strong voice.

Susan turned, and Merton Heimrich turned with her. The woman in black stepped toward them; her stride was long. Late sixties or early seventies, Heimrich thought. And not moving like it. She made him think of a long-legged bird.

"I'm Ursula Jameson," she said. "You are Susan Upton? I don't forget faces."

"I was, Miss Jameson," Susan said. "A long time ago. I'm Susan Heimrich now. It's such a lovely party."

One can only stick to the truth so long, Merton thought. He made appropriate noises which included Ursula Jameson's name.

"I know," Miss Jameson said. "Of course I know. Your husband's some sort of a policeman."

"This is my husband, Miss Jameson," Susan said and her voice, to her husband's mild surprise, was almost as firm as Ursula Jameson's, although a great deal younger. "Inspector Heimrich, of the New York State Police." She paused for a second. "Bureau of Criminal Identification," she said.

"It says 'Faye' on the window of that shop of yours," Miss Jameson said. "F-a-y-e."

"My first husband was named Faye," Susan said. "He was a Marine Corps officer. He was killed in Korea, Miss Jameson."

20

"Pity," Miss Jameson said. Under the circumstances, Merton Heimrich thought, it was a comment somewhat ambiguous.

Miss Jameson turned partly away from them. It was, Heimrich thought, as if her nose turned and the rest of her followed it. She turned toward the tall young man and the slight and very pretty girl. She said, "You two," and the girl said, "Yes, Miss Jameson?"

Looking at the two, Heimrich had thought their smiles had relaxed somewhat and that they had moved a little closer together. But now the girl's smile was as politely fixed as before and the man's might have been stenciled on his lips.

"Susan Heimrich," Miss Jameson said. "And her husband. He's a police inspector."

The very pretty girl said, "Mrs. Heimrich. Inspector. I'm Dorothy Selby. This is my cousin, Geoffrey Rankin."

"Distant cousin," Rankin said. He had a deep, pleasant voice. "I—"

"Miss Selby's helping Artie with his book," Ursula Jameson said. "Mr. Rankin lives in New York. He's— you're a lawyer, aren't you, Rankin?"

"Yes," Rankin said. "Can I get drinks for anybody? Miss Jameson? Dot?"

He looked at his own tall glass, which was empty. He looked at the glasses in the Heimrichs' hands, which were not.

"Bourbon," Ursula said, the firmness in her voice unabated. "With a little plain water and not too much ice."

The tall young man looked down at the pretty girl.

"Scotch and soda, Jeff," Dorothy Selby said. "A weak one, please."

"All right," Geoffrey Rankin said. "Only your mother's not here." He went off from their little—and shrinking— clearing, carrying three glasses.

Dorothy looked after him and laughed lightly and turned back to the Heimrichs and Ursula Jameson.

"We probably don't make much sense," Dorothy said, primarily to Susan and Merton. "My mother doesn't much approve of drinking. And, as Jeff said, she's not here. She was dreadfully sorry, Miss Jameson. But these clients—she's in real estate, you know."

Rather suddenly, Merton Heimrich did. "In Cold Harbor," he said. "Florence Selby. That's it, isn't it? A niece of mine and her husband bought their house through her a few years ago. Mr. and Mrs. John Alden."

All party conversation is irrelevant to everything. Dorothy said, "Yes?" in a voice of great politeness, which seemed to ask Heimrich to go on with a fascinating conversation.

Heimrich looked down at Susan for rescue. Susan said, "Mr. Jameson is writing a book?"

"No fool like an old fool," Ursula Jameson said to that, or apparently to that. "About time to get people to start eating."

With that she went away, toward her brother, still waiting at the double doors for late-comers, but waiting now in a small group.

They watched Ursula Jameson, her black dress whipping around a rather bony figure, as she walked toward Arthur Jameson and his little group. She walked with long strides.

"She's a dear, really," Dorothy said. "She does rather mother him, I suppose. Although actually she's a couple of years younger. Yes, Mrs. Heimrich, Mr. Jameson's writing a book. I do typing for him. Shorthand when he wants to dictate. It's about the Jamesons. They came from England in the sixteen hundreds and had a tremendous land grant. Cold Harbor was part of it. It reached almost down to Van Brunt, actually. Not quite, but almost. The first Jameson built this house. Part of it, anyway. An English family surrounded by people from Holland, they must have been."

Heimrich said, "Mmmm." Susan was more inventive. She said that it all sounded very interesting.

"Arthur thinks it is," Dorothy said. "And it really is, Mrs. Heimrich. It's going to be a very interesting book."

Methinks the lady, Heimrich thought. He looked at his glass and emptied it. He looked at Susan's, which was two-thirds emptied. "Maybe we'd better—" Heimrich said, and Geoffrey Rankin edged toward them, carrying two tall glasses and a short one on a tray. He looked at the three and said, "Miss Jameson get tired of waiting? It's rather a crush at the bar." Dorothy indicated the far end of the room with a motion of her head. Ursula had joined her brother in the little group of which he had been the center.

"Better get us refills, dear," Heimrich said to his wife. She looked up at him and then at Dorothy Selby and Geoffrey Rankin. She nodded her head slowly. They went away toward the bar.

There must be forty people in here by now, Heimrich thought. Voices were rising in the room; the room clattered with voices.

"You said we could leave early," Merton said, down to Susan and keeping his voice very low.

"Not this early," Susan said. "And probably it will thin out a little when people start to eat. They wanted to be alone. You could tell by the way they looked at each other."

"They're cousins," Heimrich said. "I do know what you mean, if you mean the pretty girl and Rankin."

"Distant cousins, he said," Susan told him. "The way we used to look at each other, I suppose."

"Right number. Wrong tense," Heimrich said, and

looked down at her. She smiled and nodded her head and said, "All right."

"And this," Heimrich said, "is sure as hell no place to be alone. Come to that, it's no place to be. Who are all these people?"

"Worthy citizens," Susan said as they moved on toward the crowded bar. "The one over there in a sort of purplish dress is Mrs. Parkins. She was in the other day looking at fabrics. She likes them purple. I don't run to purple much. And the big woman over there is Mrs. Turner. The one in the yellow dress. She redid her living room last summer. It came to yards and yards."

They managed to wedge up to the bar. There they ended beside Sam and Mary Jackson, for whom Harold was making drinks. Sam said, "Making out?" Merton Heimrich said, "Barely. Yes, Harold, when you can get to them."

Harold said, "Right up, Inspector," and filled a long glass half full of ice and measured gin onto it and flicked open a bottle of Schweppes. He mixed a martini with very little vermouth in it and poured it in a chilled glass and twisted lemon peel over it and threw the lemon peel away. The Inn is certainly going to miss him, Heimrich thought, and clicked his glass against Susan's tall glass.

"There's going to be champagne in the dining room," Harold said. "Banquet room would be more like it. Taittinger, no less. Cases of the stuff."

"That'll be nice," Susan said, with no conviction in her voice. They moved away from the bar, to make room for others who were not waiting for Taittinger. The Jacksons moved away with them.

"At eight o'clock," Sam said, "I suppose we all raise our glasses and sing, 'Happy birthday, dear Arthur.' I

24

don't know what's got into the old boy. Always been a bit of a ritualist, but all this—" He ended by shrugging his shoulders. He looked at the watch on his wrist. He said, "Fifteen minutes, I make it," and Heimrich looked at his watch and nodded his head.

"I," Mary Jackson said, "would like to sit down."

"In the First World War," Jackson said, "my father said they always synchronized their watches before they went over the top. So they would know the exact time they died, he used to say. Let's find a place to sit down."

It proved a difficult thing to do. Too many others were of the same mind. But finally they found a small sofa empty, and Mary and Susan sat on it while their two men stood in front of them. And voices clattered all around them. The voices were higher than they had been earlier. Rather shrill laughter had begun to cut through the voices. It was, Merton Heimrich decided, precisely the sort of party he liked least. The drive home would be almost thirty miles. Probably it would be raining.

"Buck up, M.L.," Sam Jackson said. "That's the old boy."

Sam Jackson, Heimrich thought, was getting a little drunk. Or perhaps it was only that his nerves were fraying.

Melodious chimes sounded, soft over the shrillness. Arthur Jameson's guests began to flow up the room toward the double open doors. Jameson himself was no longer there, nor was his sister.

"Once more into the breach," Jackson said, and held a hand down to his wife. He pulled her up beside him. The four of them joined the slow current which flowed up the room. "It's like a procession," Susan said. "In some medieval pageant."

25

"Enter lords and ladies of the court," Heimrich said, and put his empty glass down on a convenient table. Susan put hers down. With the Jacksons a few steps ahead, and the speed of the procession picking up a little, they reached the open doors and went into the square entrance hall they had come in through. A heavy man neither of them had ever seen before sat in one of the unrelenting wooden chairs. His eyes were closed, and his glass tilted in his hand.

They went across the entrance hall. More glass doors stood open on the far side of it. They went into another long room—as long and wide as the drawing room they had had their drinks in.

A table ran down the center, and candles flickered on it in silver candlesticks. There were candles, too, in sconces on the walls. The long table was covered with white linen which fell precisely to the floor; there was food the length of the table—food in bowls of ice, on platters, in warming trays. As they came through the doorway, men in white jackets held silver trays out to them, and champagne bubbled gently in the glasses on the trays. Two men in white aprons and chef's caps stood, seemingly at attention, near each of the long walls. Nobody was taking food from the long table. Everybody was waiting for something.

From behind a screen at the far end of the room, music filtered out, softly—the music of a violin and a piano.

The guests who had preceded the Heimrichs into this room—this banquet hall—stood near the walls and sipped from their glasses. After the earlier chatter over their drinks, they were strangely quiet. They were all looking toward the far end of the table, where Arthur Jameson stood, tall and slender and, Heimrich thought, almost obtrusively immaculate. He stood and smiled and waited.

And Dorothy Selby, slender in her sleeveless white dress, and looking very young, stood beside him.

When all the guests were inside—there must be forty or more, Heimrich thought—the doors to the entrance hall were closed behind them. For a few seconds, Jameson still stood erect and smiling. The slim girl beside him smiled too.

The music stopped. Then Jameson spoke; his voice projected only slightly.

"Friends," Jameson said. "Very dear friends. I have asked you here to join me in celebrating my good fortune —my most extremely good fortune. Dorothy here has done me the honor—the very great honor—to consent to become my wife."

Then he leaned down and kissed Dorothy Selby on the lips.

For a moment there was complete silence in the room. Then people began to clap their hands, and then the guests began to surge down toward Jameson and the girl. By candlelight, Heimrich thought, Jameson looked older than he had before. And Dorothy Selby looked younger.

The music started up again. The men in chef's caps moved away from the wall to the long table, and one of them began to carve a turkey. Another began to slice a ham, and a third lifted a silver ladle over something which simmered in a tureen. The fourth took up knife and fork and began to carve something on an enormous platter halfway down the table.

Heimrich looked over heads.

The man was carving a suckling pig. The pig had an apple in its mouth.

For God's sake, Heimrich thought, and followed Susan to plates and silverware on a table which crossed the long table at the near end of it.

A man in a white jacket began to snap open small

tables and set them along the walls. Another man brought chairs for them. Guests began to pick up plates and knives and forks and intricately folded napkins.

But nobody sang "Happy birthday, dear Arthur." There wasn't even a birthday cake. There would, Heimrich thought, have been too many candles.

3

It had been only a little after eleven when they got home. It had not been raining on the drive home. Merton had tipped Teddy Carnes a dollar for the car parking, and Susan had thought that too much—had thought that if others were as generous, Teddy would be on his way to another, and even noisier, Honda. But Heimrich avoids carrying silver. It jingles in the pocket. They had driven almost ten miles on their way home before either of them said anything.

This is not unusual when the Heimrichs are driving, particularly when they are driving at night—most particularly after Merton Heimrich has had a drink or two. His observation of the road ahead is then intent and unwavering. Susan sometimes helps him watch it. They had driven ten miles when Susan looked at the big man beside her, who did not look away from the road.

"There is only one word for it," Susan said. "The word is 'preposterous.'"

Heimrich did not take his eyes from the road. He said, " 'Archaic'?"

"If you'd rather," Susan said. "Perhaps 'unbelievable'? The whole thing, I mean. That poor girl."

Heimrich said, "Mmmm." For five miles he did not say anything else. Then he said, "She won't be. Poor, I mean."

Susan waited some time before answering. She waited another three miles or so. Then she said, "I suppose so. She seemed like a nice child, but I suppose so. Her family's as good as his, or almost, but that doesn't count any more."

"But not as well off," Heimrich said. He switched the heater on in the Buick. "As for the other, I'd guess it counts with Jameson. Counts one hell of a lot. Did you see the coat of arms on the wall at the end of the lounge?"

"Yes," Susan said. "A leopard rampant on what looked like a field of daisies. Or was it couchant? Or was it a field of marigolds? All that and a wing collar too. How old did Sam say he was?"

"Seventy-three," Heimrich said. "Or perhaps seventy-two. He's what they call well preserved."

"That's the word we were looking for," Susan said. " 'Preserved.' In amber, whatever that may mean. Or, 'fossilized'?"

Heimrich agreed with an "Mmmm." He drove on, at not much over forty miles an hour. Several cars passed him. He does not mind being passed on the road. He turned off NY 11F into High Road and drifted up it. The Buick climbed up the steep driveway. It was much cooler when they got out of the car. The chaises and tables on the terrace looked forsaken. They seemed, Susan thought, to be shivering.

A fire was laid in the living room, but they did not

light it. It was warm in the low house, and Heimrich turned down the thermostat. He said, "Nightcap?" but there was no enthusiasm in his voice.

"Another word could be 'exhausting,'" Susan said. "And—perhaps 'upsetting' is still another. I think the really pertinent word is 'bed.' And tomorrow's Sunday, and we can sleep late."

They went to their beds. Merton waited until he heard Susan's soft sleep-breathing before he accepted sleep. Sometimes when Susan has found an evening upsetting she lies awake. She did not that night.

Merton Heimrich dreamed, which he does not often do. The dreams were confused and meaningless. Arthur Jameson was briefly in one of the dreams. He was wearing a crown. Jameson, under his crown, said something. At first Heimrich, in his dream, could not hear the words. Then they came to him. "*Droit du seigneur*" was what the dream king said. Which was as absurd as all the rest of the dream. Then the dream Jameson began to bang a sword against a metal shield. The banging was very loud.

It became the telephone clattering between their beds.

"No. Oh—*no!*" Susan said, her voice misty.

Heimrich grabbed the telephone before it rang again. He said, "Heimrich," in a hostile voice at the same time he looked at the watch on his wrist. It was a quarter of nine. So much for their sleeping late on a Sunday morning. Heimrich said, "Yes, Charlie? I know you are. Go ahead."

He listened while Charles Forniss went ahead. He said, "With a *what?*" and went on listening. He said, "As soon as I can make it, yes," and put the receiver back in its cradle. Susan was sitting up in bed and looking at him and shaking her head slowly. There was a kind of hopelessness in the movement of her head.

31

When Heimrich spoke he realized that his fuzzy voice came from the memory of a dream.

"The king is dead," Merton told his wife, who opened her eyes widely and then, involuntarily, her mouth.

"I'm sorry," Merton said. "Somebody's killed Arthur Jameson. By shooting an arrow into his throat."

"An—a what?"

"Yes," Heimrich told her, as he swung long legs out of bed. "I did say 'arrow.' Charlie's there. At the house. He says Jameson was in a boat."

"A barge," Susan said. "To go with everything else, it would have to be a barge. I'll get the coffee going. And—" Standing beside her bed in a nightgown Heimrich could—pleasantly—see through, she shivered. "And light the fire," Susan said.

Heimrich ran an electric razor over his face. He decided to forego a shower. He dressed quickly. Flames were leaping in the fireplace when he got to the living room, and the Chemex was on a table in front of the fire, with cups and a cream pitcher beside it.

"I'm scrambling eggs," Susan said from the kitchen. "And making toast."

"I don't—" Heimrich said.

"You certainly do," Susan told him, and he did not argue. He had half finished a cup of coffee when Susan, in a quilted robe by now, brought in a tray. There was only one plate of scrambled eggs on the tray—that and toast cut into triangles. Heimrich said, "Yours?"

"Later," Susan said, and put the tray down and sat on the other side of the table and poured coffee into the other cup. "You really did say 'arrow'? As in 'bow and arrow'?"

"What Charlie told me," Heimrich said, and began to eat scrambled eggs and toast. "He just got there. I

32

suppose a bow entered into it. Or, naturally, he could just have been stabbed with an arrow, I suppose."

"In a boat," Susan said. She lighted a cigarette. She shook her head. "What was he doing in a boat at—at the crack of dawn?"

"From what Forniss has picked up, he was fishing," Heimrich said.

Susan looked across the table at him. She shook her head again. She said, "In the moat, I suppose."

Heimrich choked slightly as he finished his coffee.

"I'm sorry, darling," Susan said. "It just—well, it just seemed fitting somehow."

"Yes," Heimrich said and stood up. "No. It seems The Tor comes complete with private lake."

Susan stood up too. He kissed her. She said, "Wear a coat, dear. It's got much colder."

Heimrich put a coat on before he went out of the house. Susan was right. It had got much colder. It wasn't at all like summer any more.

It was still colder on The Tor's high hill when he got there, which he did in about forty minutes.

There were three State Police cruisers in the parking area. A trooper in uniform stood by one of them and came to Heimrich's Buick as Heimrich got out of it. He saluted. He said, "They're around back, Inspector." He pointed. He said, "That way, sir. Want I should show you? Only the doctor hasn't showed up yet, and the lieutenant said I should wait for him."

"I'll find the way," Heimrich said.

The big fieldstone house, from which light had streamed the night before, seemed sullen now. It cast a heavy black shadow across the turnaround. Heimrich walked through the shadow around the house, following a brick pathway which led across a flagstone terrace.

33

He came into sunlight and to a flight of brick stairs leading down. Some distance below, the early sunlight glinted on water.

The brick staircase was steep. There was a handrail and, going down the stairs cautiously, Heimrich used it for guidance. It was a long way down; finally the glint of sunlight on water shaped itself into a lake.

It was a larger lake than one would have expected so high in hills. It was irregular in shape. A spring-fed brook dammed into a lake? Heimrich wondered. Or a lake entirely artificial, fed from deep wells? Perhaps four hundred yards long by two hundred wide, but kidney-shaped because a promontory jutted into it—a tongue of wooded land reaching well out into the water. Four men stood at the end of the tongue of land. Two of them wore waders up almost to their hips, and one of the booted men was Lieutenant Charles Forniss, New York State Police. Two of the others were uniformed troopers. The fourth man, in boots and wearing a windbreaker, was as tall as Forniss. The four stood near the end of the spit, and all looked toward the lake.

The staircase ended at the promontory, and until he had walked fifty feet out on it, still on a well-kept path, Heimrich could not see what the four men were looking at. Forniss heard his footfalls on the paved pathway and turned and said, "Morning, M.L. We've been waiting."

Heimrich went on and joined the four. The fourth man, the one in the boots and windbreaker, was Geoffrey Rankin, the "distant" cousin of the pretty girl who had been going to marry Arthur Jameson. Rankin said, "Morning, Inspector. It's a hell of a thing."

Heimrich went on until he saw the hell of a thing. It was a rowboat. It was a light rowboat, the oars still in the locks. A man had fallen from the rower's seat and lay sprawled in the bottom of the boat, his head against the stern thwart. There was blood on the thwart. A narrow shaft was sticking out of the man's neck, and there were feathers on the end of the shaft. The sprawled man had on a turtleneck sweater and what appeared to be corduroy trousers.

"Jameson," Forniss said. "Been out fishing. There are four bass in the creel. It's shallow there and we could wade out—Mr. Rankin here and I. The boat's where it was when Mr. Rankin found it. Apparently he was rowing in when it hit him. Planning to tie the boat up, at a guess. There."

He pointed to planks which reached out into the water from the end of the spit of land. The planks were supported by heavy piles driven into the lake bed.

"The boat hasn't drifted?" Heimrich asked.

"Swung a little," Forniss said. "Mr. Rankin and I tied a line to it and a chunk of rock at the other end. I thought you'd want to see it where we—where Mr. Rankin here—says it was when he first saw it. It's about fifteen feet from the dock. The arrow's gone in near the back of the neck, a little to the left of the spinal column. Where it would hit if he was rowing in and the person who shot the arrow was standing about—oh, about where we are. On the path, at a guess. Anyway, we haven't found any footprints beside the path. Of course, the ground's pretty dry."

"It's a steel arrow," Rankin said. "The kind some of them are nowadays. It's short. Not over two feet. Probably came from a light bow. I'm just guessing, of course. Maybe not more than thirty pounds weight."

"The bow weighed thirty pounds?" Heimrich said. "Sounds pretty heavy to me."

"Not the bow itself," Rankin said. "Thirty-pound pull to draw the arrow. No good for distance, of course. Not the kind a man'd use for hunting. The way they do in Westchester."

Heimrich knew that, for part of the deer season in Westchester County, only bows and arrows were permitted weapons for deer hunters. He did not approve. Deer frequently live a long time with arrows in them; live long enough for wild dogs to get them.

"You've got pictures?" Heimrich said, and Forniss pointed to one of the troopers, who said, "Yes, we have, Inspector. From here."

"All right, Charlie," Heimrich said. "I've seen it. You can haul it in. Since you're the one with boots on."

Forniss waded out. The water came up only to his calves. He reached down and, through the clear water, Heimrich could see him freeing a stone which had been tied to the rope. With the stone off, Forniss used the rope to drag the boat to the dock. He looped the rope around one of the piles and made a hitch in it.

Heimrich walked out on the planking and looked down into the boat. Jameson's head was twisted on the aft thwart so that Heimrich could see the face in profile. It was Jameson's face, all right. Jameson hadn't shaved before he went fishing.

"Go ahead," Heimrich told the trooper who had taken the pictures, and got out of the way. The trooper took a camera out of his tunic pocket and began shooting down into the boat.

"The doctor'll want to see him the way he is," Forniss said, needlessly. "Yes," Heimrich said, also needlessly.

"All right, Mr. Rankin," Heimrich said. "Suppose you tell us about it? About finding Mr. Jameson in the boat. When did you find him, by the way?"

"At a little before eight, probably."

"You came down to join him? To go fishing with him?"

"No. I couldn't sleep. I—I was just out for a walk. I woke up at five and couldn't get back to sleep."

"You'd spent the night here, I gather," Heimrich said. "Here at Mr. Jameson's house?"

It had worked out that way, Rankin said. He had planned to stay at an inn outside Cold Harbor where he had a reservation for the weekend. "Had my overnight bag in the car. But it had got sort of late. And I'd had quite a bit to drink. And Jameson made rather a point of my staying on. Said there was all the room in the world. That sort of thing. So—I said all right. But then I woke up early and—well, got up and went out for a walk. And I thought I might as well go down and look at this lake Dot—Miss Selby, that is—had told me about. He'd talked about it a lot to her, apparently. Was damn proud of it, I gathered from what she said."

"Did Miss Selby say Mr. Jameson was in the habit of going fishing in the early mornings?"

"No. Only that he'd had the lake stocked. Every spring, she said. Ever since he had the dam put in. Something his ancestors hadn't gotten around to, apparently."

Heimrich said he saw. He said, "Were there other overnight guests last night, Mr. Rankin?"

"I don't know you'd call them guests, exactly," Rankin said. "Ronnie stayed over. And the Tennants. They were here for the weekend. Family, rather than guests. Although Ronnie and the Tennants live in the city."

Heimrich repeated, "Family?"

"Ronald Jameson," Rankin said. "The old man's—I mean Arthur Jameson's—son by his first marriage. And

Estelle Tennant is his daughter by the second. Second marriage, that is. Her husband's James Tennant. He's a psychiatrist. Dr. James Tennant."

Heimrich said he saw. He said, "And Miss Jameson, naturally."

Rankin said, "Sure. She lives here."

"Miss Selby?"

"No. Actually, Dot has a room here. Sometimes she stayed overnight when Jameson wanted to work late. On this book about the family. Last night she didn't. Her mother came and got her. Very vigorous woman, Mrs. Selby. About eleven she drove up. Party'd pretty much broken up by then. There were a few people still around and Miss Jameson. The old man was in what he calls—called—his office with this lawyer of his. I don't know the fella's name."

"Jackson," Heimrich said. "The others were just—sitting around?"

"Getting their coats, mostly. Half a dozen or so. People who live nearby, I'd guess. And Mrs. Selby stalked in. Said something like, 'Come on, Dorothy. It's time to go home.' Something like that. I don't know why I said, 'stalked.' She's a little, round sort of woman. She just walked in, of course. But she—well, she wasn't wasting any time. She was sort of abrupt about it."

Merton Heimrich said, "Abrupt?"

"The way it felt to me. But you don't care how things felt to me, I suppose."

"I'm interested in anything you can tell me," Heimrich said. "As if she objected to her daughter's staying in Mr. Jameson's house? But you say she had before."

"I don't know," Rankin said. "Of course, after the old boy announced the engagement—pretty theatrical about it, wasn't he?—Flo may have figured that the situation had changed. Staying over as Jameson's secretary was one thing. As his fiancée another. You'll have to ask Flo herself, Inspector. She—"

He broke off. A short, firm man was coming down the steep brick staircase. He was coming carefully. He carried a black bag. "Dr. Fleming." Forniss said.

Dr. Curtis Fleming is, when called upon, a police surgeon. He represents the coroner, an official which Putnam County still prefers to a medical examiner. They watched Dr. Fleming come down the stairs and along the brick path. When he was close enough, Fleming said, "Hell of a time on a Sunday morning. Where is it?"

They showed him where it was.

"All right," Fleming said. "Somebody get it out. I'm not going down into that damn boat. Morning, M.L. I suppose you've taken all the pretty pictures you want." Dr. Fleming looked down into the boat. He said, "An arrow, for God's sake! Indians around?"

"We don't know who was around, Doctor," Heimrich said.

The troopers got the body of Arthur Jameson out of the boat and laid it on the dock planking. Fleming crouched down beside the body. He moved the body's arms; he looked into the blank eyes. He said, "All right to take this damn thing out? Because he won't be bleeding any more."

Heimrich said it was all right to take the damn thing out, and Dr. Fleming pulled the arrow from the dead man's neck. It came out easily; it came out bloody.

"Not very deep," Dr. Fleming said, and got a probe out of his bag and inserted it into the round hole the arrow had made in Jameson's neck. "Deep enough," Fleming said. "Pierced one of the carotids, apparently. We'll know better when we take it apart."

"How long, Doctor?" Heimrich asked.

"Two, three hours, at a guess. No rigor yet. We'll have to get it down to the hospital at Cold Harbor." He stood up; he looked at the steep brick staircase. "Somebody will," Dr. Fleming said. He walked away and started up the stairs.

"We've already called for an ambulance," Forniss said. "They'll have a stretcher."

"We may as well go up to the house," Heimrich said. "Warmer inside. After you found the body, Mr. Rankin. Did you tell the others? His sister and daughter and son?"

"I just went back up to the house and found a telephone," Rankin said. "I don't know whether anybody else was up. Oh, one of the maids was dusting things. She may have heard me call the police."

"Called them and then came back down here?" Heimrich said.

"Got a pair of boots and came back," Rankin said. "Waded out and—well, looked at him. I was pretty sure he was dead but—hell, he might not have been."

"Did you touch Mr. Jameson's body, Mr. Rankin? Move it in any way?"

"No. Looking was enough. At him and—and at all that blood."

"We'll go on up," Heimrich said. "Tell the family. You, Trooper—" He looked at the trooper who had taken the photographs. "What's your name, by the way?"

"Carnes, Inspector. Robert Carnes, sir."

"Any relation to Teddy Carnes? The Van Brunt Teddy Carnes?"

"He's sort of a cousin, sir."

"All right. Get the shots printed up. Put them in my —no, bring them back here. We'll be here quite a while, probably."

40

Trooper Carnes said, "Sir," and that he'd have to go up to Troop K to do the developing.

Rankin and Heimrich and Forniss and the two troopers climbed the brick staircase and went to the front door of The Tor. It was closed and locked. "I went out the back," Rankin said. "Quickest way. We can—"

But then the door opened. Ursula Jameson opened it. She was lean and tall in black slacks and a black sweater. Her white hair looked as if she had combed it with her fingers. Her long, tanned and wrinkled face looked older than it had the night before. Her eyes were wide and staring.

Geoffrey Rankin was nearest her, but she looked at Heimrich, not at Rankin.

"You're that inspector," she said. "You were here last night. Something's happened. *Hasn't something happened?*"

"Yes," Heimrich said. "Something's happened, Miss Jameson. Perhaps we'd better go in and sit down."

She stood motionless in the doorway. Her hands began to move, as if they were clutching at something.

"I heard somebody coming," she said. "I thought it was Arthur, at first, but he wouldn't bring his fish in this way. He never does. He takes them—" She stopped speaking and began to move her head from side to side.

"We'd better go inside," Heimrich said.

"It's Arthur, isn't it? Something's happened to Arthur. *That's what it is, isn't it?*"

"Yes," Heimrich said. "Something's happened to your brother, Miss Jameson. I'm afraid—"

And then he moved quickly and caught her as she swayed. He had thought she would be frail in his hands, but the old body was firm, muscled.

Ursula Jameson's body tightened. "I'm all right," she

41

said. "All *right*. He's dead, isn't he? That's what you're trying to tell me, isn't it? That Arthur's dead."

"Yes, Miss Jameson," Heimrich said. "I'm afraid it is."

"But he was a good swimmer," Ursula Jameson said. "When we were young he used to win all the prizes."

She turned then, and they followed her into the square entrance hall and then into the long drawing room where the party had started. There were no signs left of the party. The bar from which Harold had served drinks was gone from the end of the long room. A fire was burning in the big fireplace. It was a beginning fire, with flames still leaping up from kindling under four big logs.

Ursula Jameson sat on a sofa in front of the fire. She gestured toward chairs, and Heimrich and Forniss pulled chairs toward the sofa, at opposite ends. Rankin continued to stand. He said, "Maybe I'd better—" and let it hang.

"No, Mr. Rankin," Heimrich said. "There're one or two more things you can tell me."

Rankin pulled up a chair and sat between Heimrich and the fire.

"Of course," Ursula Jameson said, "the water would have been cold. Perhaps he got a cramp. That must have been the way—"

"No," Heimrich said. "Your brother didn't drown, Miss Jameson. He—somebody shot him. With an arrow. From the bank, apparently. As he was bringing the boat in."

She looked at him blankly for a moment. Then she said, "An *arrow*? You said an *arrow*? You mean, somebody killed him?"

"Yes, Miss Jameson," Heimrich said. "I'm afraid that's the way it was. Somebody who knew he'd gone out fishing. Who would have known that?"

She said, "Known what?" and her voice, which had

been strong before, was vague. For a moment she covered her long face with thin, mottled hands. Then she said, "Everybody, I guess. Everybody who knows us. Every Sunday morning he went out early to catch fish for breakfast. Unless the weather was very bad, of course. It was—it was a kind of ritual with my brother. For years he's caught us fish for Sunday breakfast. He cooked them himself, because he could never find anybody else who could do them the right way. Myrtle does everything else very well but she's never got the knack of doing fish the way he likes them. And Ellen couldn't either. She was the one before Myrtle. Not even Reynolds, and he'd been a chef in the city before he came here."

"Always at about the same time, Miss Jameson?"

"Oh, even earlier in the summer, of course. Because it gets light so much earlier. He's always thought fish bite better early in the morning. And of course he keeps the lake well stocked. You're sure it was an arrow?"

"Yes," Heimrich said. "A metal arrow. Was Mr. Jameson interested in archery?"

"A long time ago," she said. "He used to shoot at targets. He tried to teach me, but I could never hit anything. But that was a long time ago. He got tired of it, after a while. Then he took up golf. He's always been like that, you see. Active. Even as he gets older, he's always doing things."

Tenses are tricky when a man is dead, Heimrich thought. The past tense comes slowly and comes hard.

Ursula Jameson seemed to hear her own words.

"I talk as if he were still alive," she said. "And you say he's dead. You say somebody killed him. Who would do that, Inspector? Who would do a thing like that?"

Then she got up from the sofa and walked away. She

43

walked stiffly. Forniss looked at Heimrich and Heimrich shook his head. When Ursula Jameson had gone between the big double doors at the upper end of the room and out into the entrance hall, Heimrich said, "Later, Charlie."

Heimrich turned to Rankin.

"Down by the lake," he said, "you talked as if you knew something about archery, Mr. Rankin. Do you go in for it yourself?"

4

Geoffrey Rankin did not answer the question directly. Instead he said, "Has either of you got a cigarette?" Heimrich produced a pack of cigarettes and held it out to Rankin. Rankin took a cigarette from the pack and said, "And a match?" Heimrich flicked flame into his lighter and held it out, and Rankin drew fire into his cigarette and breathed smoke in and let it out.

"There's an old saying," Rankin said. "Something like 'A lawyer who represents himself has a fool for a client.' I'm a lawyer, Inspector. This morning I couldn't sleep, and it looked from the window like being a nice day, so I went down the back stairs and out onto the terrace. Through there." He pointed to french doors at the far end of the room. "I decided to go down and look at this lake of the old boy's. I found his body. I called the police. A lawyer would advise me to say 'period' at that point."

"It's up to you," Heimrich said. "You don't have to answer any questions that bother you."

"When I was in my late teens," Rankin said, "my people had a place on Long Island. My father had an archery range. He was quite good at it, in an amateur sort of way. We shot at targets, not at people. I gave it up when I was—oh, about eighteen. It bored me. Tennis didn't." Again he drew deeply on his cigarette. "I wasn't too good at tennis, either, but I liked to play it."

Heimrich nodded his head to show he was listening. He closed his eyes so that he could listen better. Rankin said, "Am I putting you to sleep, Inspector?" and Heimrich said, "No, Mr. Rankin. You do know something about archery, then?"

"Very little," Rankin said. "As I said, it bored me. That the 'weight' of a bow is the poundage it takes to pull the arrow to the tip. I didn't bring a bow and arrow up here in my pocket, Inspector. Awkward thing to carry around, a bow. Noticeable. Also, I didn't know about Jameson's habit of catching fish on Sunday mornings for breakfast. Or about his having some special way of cooking them."

"Some modern bows are jointed," Forniss said. "They can be put together through a metal sleeve, like a fishing pole."

"That so?" Rankin said. "My father's weren't. They were about five feet long and made of yew. The arrows were made of wood, metal-tipped. The bows weighed thirty pounds, my father told me. After he died, my mother gave them away to somebody. Perhaps to the local thrift shop. Again, I didn't bring one with me. I didn't kill the old boy, either."

"All right," Heimrich said. "You didn't bring a bow and arrows with you. Did you bring Miss Selby?"

"As a matter of fact—" Rankin said and then stopped

46

and looked at Heimrich. His eyes were, Heimrich thought, a little narrowed. He said, after the pause, "Getting at something, Inspector?"

"Just trying to get the picture," Heimrich said.

"There isn't any picture," Rankin said. "None I'm in, anyway. I got an invitation to this party by mail at my apartment in New York. Surprised hell out of me. I didn't know the Jamesons. Oh, I knew Dot had been working for the old boy on this damn-fool book of his. So I called her up and asked her what the hell. She said Jameson had asked her if there was anyone she'd like to have invited to the birthday party and that she had suggested me. I said I didn't even know where Jameson's place was and she suggested I pick her up and that she'd guide me. So I did. I followed her car up here."

"To a birthday party," Heimrich said. "Miss Selby didn't tell you it was to be—well, more than that?"

"No."

The word came in a flat voice. Rankin drew on his cigarette again and then crushed it out in an ashtray. Heimrich held his pack out again, and Rankin shook his head. Merton Heimrich looked at the cigarette pack as if he had never seen one before. Then he took a cigarette out of the pack and lighted it for himself.

"I gathered last night that you and Miss Selby are cousins," Heimrich said. "Distant cousins, I think you said."

"Yes." In the same flat voice.

"And friends, I gather?"

"We saw each other now and then. Not much the last year or two."

"This relationship between the two of you," Heimrich said. "How distant is it, Mr. Rankin?"

"Miles," Rankin said. "Her mother and mine were— oh, second cousins. I think that was it. I don't know what that makes Dot and me. Not consanguineous within any reasonable—or legal—meaning. Is that what you're getting at, Inspector? Or—all right, I see. You don't need to tell me. Dot's a damn pretty kid. A damn sweet kid. Did I kill Jameson because she was going to marry him? Is that what's on your mind?"

"Just trying to get the picture," Heimrich said again. "Last night you and Miss Selby seemed to be—oh, getting along pleasantly enough together. Rather enjoyed being together, it seemed to me."

"What seems to you isn't evidence, is it?"

"No."

"So, you're not getting any picture. Not the kind you seem to want."

"Mr. Rankin, I don't want anything. Except to find out who killed Mr. Jameson."

Rankin didn't say anything for some seconds. Then he said, "Can I bum another cigarette?"

He got another cigarette and a light for it. He drew on it.

"If I had a lawyer," Rankin said, "he'd probably tell me to keep my mouth shut."

"You can if you want to."

"If I've got something to hide," Rankin said. "Am I still beating my wife."

"If you want to put it that way," Heimrich said. "I take it you haven't got a wife to beat, Mr. Rankin."

"No."

"There are a couple more things I'd like to ask you," Heimrich said. "You can answer or not as you like."

"Ask and you'll find out," Rankin told him. But his voice was no longer hard. He seemed more relaxed.

"You said Miss Selby's mother 'stalked' in last night," Heimrich said. "That she was 'abrupt.' With her daughter, I gathered."

48

"Did I say that? Use those words?"

"Yes."

"If I did, they were much too strong. Flo's—well, Flo's very businesslike. She's a sweet person, actually, but sometimes—well, sometimes she puts people off a bit."

"You speak as if you know her rather well, Mr. Rankin."

"Moderately. She used to come out to my parents' place when I was a kid. When Dot was just toddling around. Before Selby died. She's had—well, it was tough going for her for a while, I think. And she wouldn't take any help from anybody. At least, I think that. I was just a kid, as I said. Maybe I just imagined things, the way kids do."

"Miss Selby was just toddling around when you were a kid," Heimrich said. "About how old is Miss Selby now?"

"Around twenty-four. Twenty-five."

"And you?"

"Thirty my last birthday. And, yes, I know, Inspector. Jameson was in his seventies. But it was up to them, wasn't it?"

"Obviously. But did Mrs. Selby think so, do you know? That it was up to them?"

"I've no idea."

"Did you, Mr. Rankin?"

Rankin had only half finished his cigarette. He crushed it out abruptly.

"I think," Geoffrey Rankin said, "that I'll take my attorney's advice, Inspector."

Heimrich told Rankin it was up to him. And thought himself adequately answered.

"Then," Rankin said, "it will be all right if I get myself a cup of coffee? I could do with one."

"Yes. I'd like you to stick around, though. There may be other questions."

Geoffrey Rankin said he was damn sure there would be. He rose and walked up the long room and into the entrance hall.

"On the make for this girl he calls Dot?" Forniss said. "The girl who was going to marry Jameson?"

"She's a very pretty girl," Heimrich said. "If he's telling the truth, they're not too closely related."

"Hell," Forniss said, "first cousins get together."

"Yes," Heimrich said. "It's not recommended, but yes. I suppose we'd better—"

He stopped. A man in a sports shirt and a tweed jacket and gray slacks came into the room through the doorway at the far end, where the bar had been the night before. He had bristling black hair and was heavy and walked heavily. He also walked with vigor. He was, Heimrich guessed, about fifty. He spoke when he was halfway up the room. His voice was as heavy as his movements. He said, "What's this Aunt Ursula tells me, huh? She got things mixed up somehow, didn't she? I'm Ronald Jameson. Who are you two?"

He walked between Forniss and Heimrich and sat, heavily, on the sofa his aunt had sat on. He said, "Well?"

"Police," Heimrich said.

"Wait a minute," Ronald Jameson said. "Just wait a minute. Weren't you here last night at the party? Inspector somebody or other?"

Heimrich supplied his name. He supplied Charles Forniss's name. He said, "No, your aunt didn't get things mixed up, Mr. Jameson. If she told you your father's been killed she didn't mix anything up."

"She says with an arrow," Jameson said. "That's crazy."

He was truculent. Shock, Heimrich thought, affects different people in different ways. Ronald Jameson did not have the somewhat elaborate grace his father had had. On the other hand, he did not have his aunt's nose.

50

"Your father was shot in the neck with an arrow," Heimrich said. "He was in a boat on the lake. He'd been fishing. The arrow was made of steel. Do you know whether there are bows and arrows around here, Mr. Jameson? Around The Tor?"

"God knows what's around here," Jameson said. "All the junk in the world, for all I know. Jamesons have been accumulating stuff for generations. The attics are full of stuff. There's a storeroom in the cellar stacked with boxes. In what, I guess, used to be a wine cellar. There could be bows and arrows. There could be damn near anything."

"Do you live here, Mr. Jameson?"

"Good God, no. I live in the city. Work in the city. You think I'd stay cooped up here?"

"Well," Heimrich said, "it's a pretty large coop, Mr. Jameson. You did live here at one time? Grew up here, I suppose?"

"Until they sent me away to prep school," Jameson said. "Groton, it was. Supposed to be like father, like son. Only they threw me out of Groton. Decided I wasn't the right kind of Jameson. So I went to Dartmouth instead of Harvard. Upset the old man. He used to rag me about it. So when I got out of college I didn't come back here. My mother was dead by then. There wasn't any point in living here. Trying to be the kind of Jameson my father wanted. See what I mean?"

"Your mother was Mr. Jameson's first wife, I take it?" Heimrich said.

"Rebecca Jameson," Ronald Jameson said. "She died when I was at college. She'd—well, she'd been sick a long time."

There was a change in Jameson's voice. Much of the harshness went out of it. There was a kind of sadness in the heavy voice.

51

"If she'd had the right kind of—" he said, in the softened voice. He did not finish the sentence. "Thing was, I guess, she wasn't the right kind of Jameson either."

He turned suddenly on the sofa and looked toward the outside wall of the room, where curtained french doors opened onto a terrace. He said, "There she is. Want to see her?" and got up from the sofa and went around it and across the room. Heimrich went after him. "There," Ronald Jameson said, and pointed.

He pointed at a portrait on the wall between the french doors. He reached out and touched a switch, and a light came on under the portrait.

It was a portrait of a woman. She had been painted in evening dress, her shoulders bare. Dark hair, cut short in the manner of the late twenties, curled softly around her face.

"Beautiful, wasn't she?" Jameson said. "Painted when I—oh, I suppose I couldn't have been more than five or six. I remember her like that when I was older. Before she got sick. The old man got a good man to paint her, didn't he? She was beautiful, wasn't she?"

"Yes," Heimrich said.

"He was proud of her then, I guess," Jameson said. "A fine possession, worthy of a Jameson. And he let her die."

"People die," Heimrich said. "People don't let them die."

"Have it your own way," Jameson said, and, abruptly, turned off the light under the portrait. He walked back toward the sofa in front of the fire, which now was burning steadily. He sat down on the sofa and looked into the fire.

"It's your father's death we're interested in," Heimrich said.

"Just as he was about to become a happy bridegroom

again," Jameson said. "To a girl who, from the looks of her, could be his granddaughter. My stepmother—Janet—was about that age when he married her. And he—hell, he must have been damn near as old as I am now. He likes them young." He paused. "Liked them young," he said. "I keep forgetting. I'm not talking—not acting —the way a bereaved son ought to. That's what you're thinking, isn't it?"

It was, but there was not much point in saying so.

"I'm trying to find out who killed your father," Heimrich said.

"And thinking maybe I did? That won't get you anywhere, Inspector. We weren't close, as I suppose you think all fathers and sons ought to be. There's no law requiring that, is there? I came out here for his birthday party. He invited me. I was filial enough to come. I didn't come out here to kill him. Also, I never used a bow and arrow in my life. Wouldn't have any idea how to go about it."

"All right," Heimrich said. "You say your father liked them young. Since he was a good deal older than your stepmother. A lot older than Miss Selby. Did you know he planned to marry Miss Selby?"

"No. I just thought it was going to be a birthday party. Oh, I wondered a little when it turned out to be such a fancy one. I didn't know he was going to announce his engagement in that damned flossy way. To that kid. Maybe I shouldn't have been surprised. Janet was damn near twenty-five years younger than he. She was younger than I, come to that. He married her a little over a year after Mother died."

"She has died, too, Mr. Jameson? You said she 'was.'"

"Killed a couple of years ago. Nothing you'd be interested in, Inspector. Her horse fell on a jump. Threw her into a stone fence and it broke her neck. She was

Estelle's mother. Estelle and her husband are here in the house. Did you know that, Inspector?"

"Yes."

"Has anybody told her about this?"

"Your aunt may have," Heimrich said. "When did you wake up this morning, Mr. Jameson?"

"When Aunt Ursula banged on the door and told me about Father."

"You hadn't heard anything before that? Anybody moving around? Your father went out early to go fishing. Mr. Rankin went out somewhat later because he couldn't sleep. The servants were probably up and around earlier, clearing up after the party. You didn't hear anything? Nothing waked you up. Until your aunt knocked on the door."

"No. If there was anything going on I slept through it."

"Then I guess, for now anyway—" Heimrich said, and let it hang. He said, "By the way, Mr. Jameson. You said you work in New York. Mind telling me what kind of work?"

"Why should I? I'm a partner in an advertising agency. Jameson and Perkins. And, if you're wondering, I don't need any of the old man's money. Not that I'll get any, at a guess. The thing is, I don't need it."

"All right," Heimrich said. "That's all for now, Mr. Jameson. Only—you weren't planning to go back to the city right away, were you?"

"Am I free to?"

"Naturally, Mr. Jameson. I'd a little rather you didn't. But you won't be stopped."

"I'll be around," Jameson said, and stood up. He said, "Go easy with Sis, will you? This—well, this will shake her up pretty bad. And she's a nice kid."

54

"I go as easy as I can with everybody," Heimrich said. "I'll probably see you later, Mr. Jameson. As things come up."

They watched Jameson walk down the room, toward the door in the far wall. He seemed rather to be shouldering his way down the room.

"Seems he didn't like his old man much," Forniss said.

"And doesn't try much to hide it," Heimrich said. "I suppose we'd better talk to the daughter, Charlie. Mrs.—what did Rankin say her name was?"

"Tennant," Forniss said. "Her husband's some kind of a headshrinker. Psychiatrist, Rankin said."

"An M.D., then," Heimrich said. "Might see if you can find them, Charlie."

Forniss went to find Dr. and Mrs. Tennant. He didn't have far to go. He met a couple entering the room through the double doors and came back with them.

Estelle Tennant had black hair which lay smoothly on her head; she had large dark brown eyes. She was, Heimrich thought, in her middle twenties—about the age of the girl her father had planned to marry. Estelle Tennant had also, Heimrich thought, been crying. She was not crying as she walked down the room with her husband beside her and Forniss a step or two behind. But as she walked nearer, Heimrich could see that she was still catching her breath in sobs.

Her husband appeared to be some years older. He was taller than his slim wife, but not a great deal taller. He was, Heimrich guessed, in his late thirties or early forties. He was not dressed for the country. He wore a dark suit and a white shirt and a nonassertive dark blue necktie. He was clean-shaven, and his blond hair was short. But Heimrich is not among those who expect psychiatrists to be bearded.

Heimrich stood up as they drew near. He said, "Mrs. Tennant. Doctor."

Estelle Tennant merely nodded her head uncertainly. Dr. Tennant said, "All right, dear. Sit down." He put an arm around her shoulders and guided her to the sofa in front of the fire. He himself remained standing. He said, "You'll be Inspector Heimrich? From the police."

His voice was unexpectedly soft, almost soothing. It did not go with the outward crispness of the man. Heimrich said he was a police inspector.

"Miss Jameson felt you would want to talk to us," Dr. Tennant said. "Although I'm afraid there is nothing we can tell you. She—she is very much shaken. I suggested sedation, but she refused it. Of course, I'm not her physician. But I suppose what she told us is correct? It seems—well, it seems improbable."

"I assume she told you her brother had been killed," Heimrich said. "Shot in the neck with an arrow. It pierced a carotid artery, the police doctor says. Yes, it is an improbable way to die."

"Probably lost consciousness almost at once," Tennant said. "Bled to death."

"Don't," Estelle said, and covered her face with her hands. "Please don't, Jim. *Please!*"

Her voice shook. Tennant sat down beside her on the sofa and held her to him. She took her hands down from her face and pressed her face against his shoulder. He said, "There, dear. There, Estelle," and his arm tightened around her. He looked across at Heimrich and said, "My wife's in shock. I hope you can make this brief. I don't know how we can help you, anyway."

"Only if you heard anything this morning," Heimrich said. "People moving about. Or, of course, saw anything that may help us."

"You think whoever did this was in the house? I

mean, followed Mr. Jameson from the house? Carrying a bow and arrow? It—it sounds preposterous, Inspector. Somebody from outside? You'd thought of that?"

"Of course," Heimrich said. "It was somebody who knew Mr. Jameson was in the habit of going fishing early on Sunday mornings."

"Which hundreds of people may have known," the doctor pointed out. "Men like Jameson—well, they are celebrities in neighborhoods. People pick up things about them. The lake probably is visible for miles around. Anybody may have seen him out in this boat of his. Come to that, I've seen him myself. Not this morning. Other times Stel and I've been up here."

"Do you come here often, Doctor?"

"Every few weeks," Tennant said. "It's coming home, to my wife."

"He was my father," Estelle said, suddenly freeing herself from her husband's arm. Her voice shook. It was a light, shaking voice. "He was my *father*. You're—you're all talking about him as if—as if he were just an object. An *object!*"

Tennant drew her close to him again. She said, "Oh Jim. Jim!" He said, "There, dear. I know," and tightened his arm around her. Her face was against his shoulder again. He looked over her at Heimrich and shook his head slowly.

"Mrs. Tennant," Heimrich said, "I hate to put you through this. We don't think of your father as—as an object. We think of him as a man who has been killed. We're trying to find out who killed him. You want that, don't you?"

"He's dead," Estelle said, not moving her head from her husband's shoulder, her voice muffled. "Don't you understand he's dead?"

"She can't stand too much of this," Tennant said.

57

"If you've got questions to ask, ask them, will you? I don't know how we can help, but we want to help."

"If you heard anything this morning. Saw anything. As I said, people moving about."

"No."

"Where is your room, Doctor? The room you and Mrs. Tennant were in last night?"

"Whenever we come up here," Tennant said, "it's always the same room. It was Stel's room before we were married. They had another bed put in it when we first started to come up. Otherwise, it's much the same as it was when she lived here, I think. She says it is."

"I'm all right now," Estelle Tennant said, and sat erect again. Her husband still kept his arm around her. "They thought I would like it that way. Would feel I was coming home. It—it meant a lot to me."

"Naturally," Heimrich said.

"Father—" she said, and again her voice broke. She waited a moment. "Father thought we ought to have one of the larger rooms," she said, her voice steady again. "But Aunt Ursula said it would be more like coming home if I had the room I used to have. Grew up having."

"Yes," Heimrich said. "Where is the room, Mrs. Tennant?"

Tennant answered him. It was a corner room toward the rear of the house. "Above the terrace." In the winter, with the leaves off, one could see the lake from one of the windows. But now the leaves were only beginning to turn; now the leaves cut off the view of the lake.

"Above the terrace," Heimrich said. "The terrace runs the full depth of the house, doesn't it? Toward the rear of the house, your room is, Doctor?"

"At the far corner," Tennant said. "Above what is—

what was—Jameson's study. The room he worked in on this book of his. Back there."

He turned on the sofa, his arm still about his wife's shoulders. With his free hand he pointed down the long room, toward the door through which Ronald Jameson had recently come and gone. "Back there," he said.

"No," Estelle said. "There's another room beyond it. A kind—oh, a kind of breakfast room. It opens off the kitchen. It's where we used to have breakfast when I was a little girl. Dad and Mother and Aunt Ursula and I."

Heimrich said, "Yes, Mrs. Tennant."

"It's that room ours is really over, Jim," Estelle said. Her voice was quite steady now. "You'd forgotten that room. It wasn't used much when we had guests. And—and you and I've been guests, Jim."

"I'd forgotten," Dr. Tennant said. "She's right, of course."

"The other rooms on this side of the house," Heimrich said. "Do they all have french doors opening on the terrace, as this one has? Mr. Jameson's study? The breakfast room?"

"I think so," Tennant said.

"Of course. All of them," Estelle said. "It's—he must have been on the terrace when—when I—"

Her voice broke again, and again Tennant's arm tightened around her shoulders. Again he said, "There, dear."

A psychiatrist ought to be able to think of more soothing words, Heimrich thought. He just makes the same sounds I make when Susan's upset about something. After some seconds, Heimrich said, "When you what, Mrs. Tennant?"

"Heard his voice," Estelle said. "I know it was his

voice. We had the windows open, of course, and he must have been down on the terrace."

"When was this, Mrs. Tennant? This morning?"

"It was just beginning to get light," Estelle Tennant said. "I suppose the light woke me. I don't know what time. About seven?"

"Possibly," Heimrich said. "You heard your father speaking? From the terrace?"

"That's what I'm telling you, Inspector."

"Yes. What did he say?"

"Just, 'Good morning.'"

"Loudly? As if he knew you were awake and was saying good morning to you through the window?"

"No. As if he were speaking to somebody who was on the terrace with him."

"As if he were surprised to find somebody on the terrace? At such an early hour?"

"I don't know," Estelle said. "No, it didn't sound like that. He—he sounded gay. I don't know. Happy. He loved to go out fishing by himself early in the morning."

"You didn't get up and look down to the terrace? To see who your father was speaking to?"

"No. No! I just went back to sleep."

"You didn't hear Mr. Jameson say good morning to somebody, Doctor?"

"No. Stel's bed is nearer the window. I didn't hear anything. The light doesn't strike my bed as early as it does hers. Probably wouldn't wake me if it did. I was in general practice for some years. I learned to sleep hard when I got a chance."

Heimrich himself sleeps hard when he has a chance. He nodded his head.

"He didn't sound surprised when he said, 'Good morning,' Mrs. Tennant? Just—just cheerful?"

"Yes. The way he was in the mornings. I—I should

have looked out. I *should* have. I—I just went back to sleep. If I'd looked out I'd—I'd have seen him. I could have said, 'Hi, Dad. Catch lots of fish, Dad.' I could have—" She stopped speaking and moved her head slowly from side to side. There was, Heimrich thought, a kind of desolation in the way she moved her head.

"There, dear," Dr. Tennant said. "There, child."

5

It was unfortunate, Heimrich thought, that Estelle
Tennant had not looked down from the bedroom window;
had not seen her father or the person he had been speaking to. It was unfortunate, but it had been entirely
natural for her merely to go back to sleep. Also, the
person to whom Jameson had said good morning was
not necessarily, was not even probably, the person who
had killed him. After the encounter on the terrace, Jameson had gone down the long brick staircase to the jut
of land into the lake; he had got in a rowboat and
fished long enough to catch four bass.

"After a party like the one last night, Mrs. Tennant,"
Heimrich said, "there would have been a lot of cleaning
up to do. The staff would have been up early, probably.
Your father might have come across one of the servants
on the terrace."

She supposed so.

"Did he sound as if he were speaking to one of the servants?"

She did not know what he meant. Her father spoke to servants as he spoke to anyone else.

"He was a gentle man," she said. "A considerate man. Did you think he—he was rude to the people who worked here?"

"No," Heimrich said. "I just asked a question. With some people there is a difference in—in intonation. How many people work here in the house, do you know, Mrs. Tennant?"

She began to count, tapping the fingers of her right hand on the sofa cushion beside her. There was Myrtle, the cook. There was Barnes. "He takes—took—care of father's clothes and things like that. He answered the door, most of the time. Sometimes, when Aunt Ursula and Dad had dinner parties, he helped serve." There were two maids. One of them, she thought, was named Gladys. The other was new. "They sort of come and go." There was Frans Frankel. He was the outdoors man; the yardman. "He takes care of the boats. Things like that." There was his wife, Gretchen. "They live over the garage. Sometimes, I think, she helps out with the heavy cleaning."

It came to six, if one counted Mrs. Frankel, who only helped out sometimes.

"Last night," Estelle said, "Aunt Ursula must have got in extra people. From Cold Harbor, I guess. You'll have to ask her about that sort of thing, Inspector. She —well, she ran The Tor for Dad. Always has, I think."

"When your mother was alive? And your father's first wife?"

"I don't know, really. It—I guess it felt like that when I was a little girl. Mother was always active in the hunt club. I don't know how things were when Ron's mother was alive. Because, of course, I wasn't born then."

"We'll want to talk to the servants," Heimrich said. "See if any of them saw or heard anything this morning. Also, we'll want to go over the house. See if we can find the weapon."

"The bow somebody used," Estelle said. "That's what you want to find, isn't it?"

Heimrich said it was. He said they would need permission to search the house.

Estelle supposed it would be all right. It would be for Aunt Ursula to decide.

"If Miss Jameson paid any attention to my advice," Dr. Tennant said, "she's resting. I gave her a couple of tranquilizers. I don't know whether—" He stopped and turned so that he faced up the long room. He said, "Apparently she didn't."

Ursula Jameson, dressed in black slacks and sweater as she had been before, was walking down the room toward them. Her scanty white hair no longer looked as if she had combed it with her fingers. She walked toward them with long strides. As if, Heimrich thought, she were walking a golf course. They all watched her walking toward them. Heimrich stood up as she came near. Dr. Tennant did not; he sat beside his wife with a protective arm around her.

"Are you badgering my niece about this awful thing?" Ursula Jameson said. She stood facing Heimrich. She looked at him intently and waited intently for an answer.

"No," Heimrich said. "Do you feel I've been badgering you, Mrs. Tennant?"

Estelle said, "No, Aunt Ursula. He hasn't been."

"We have to ask questions," Heimrich said. "We have to find out what happened this morning. Whether anybody heard or saw anything that might help us. We'll want to talk to the servants, Miss Jameson. We'll want to search the house for the bow somebody used."

"You'll have men tramping all over," Ursula said. Her voice was stiff.

"Looking in likely places," Heimrich said. "By the way, can you tell me where your brother kept his fishing gear? Golf clubs, perhaps?"

"There's a closet off his office," Ursula Jameson said. "And another off the breakfast room behind the office. In one of them. Perhaps in both of them. The servants won't have heard or seen anything. What would there have been to see? My brother went early to fish. You say somebody killed him. Do you think the servants saw somebody kill him?"

"Sit down, Miss Jameson," Heimrich said. She hesitated. Heimrich indicated the chair he had been sitting in. She looked at her niece. She said, "Are you all right, child?" and the stiffness went partly out of her voice.

"She's in shock, Miss Jameson," Dr. Tennant said. "So are you, for that matter. You should have taken the medicine I gave you. You should be lying down."

Ursula Jameson said, "Nonsense." She sat down on the chair Heimrich had indicated. But then, almost at once, she stood up again. "I'll ring for Barnes," she said. "He'll get the others. I'll—"

"There's no hurry," Heimrich said. "We'll get to them later."

She sat down again.

"Mrs. Tennant heard your brother saying good morning to somebody on the terrace," Heimrich said. "She thinks probably about seven this morning. He wasn't speaking to you, I take it?"

"At seven this morning I was asleep," Ursula said. The

stiffness was back in her voice. "I didn't wake up until Joan came to tell me this Mr. Rankin was calling the police. And that it sounded as if something had happened."

Joan, Heimrich assumed, was the new maid—the maid who had overheard Rankin on the telephone. He said, "Mmmm." Then he said, "By the way, Miss Jameson. I take it your room isn't over the terrace?"

"Of course not," Ursula Jameson said, in a tone which seemed to accuse Merton Heimrich of stupidity. "On the other side of the house. The corner rooms at the back. My bedroom and dressing room, with a bath between. My brother has the same sort of rooms on the front corner. You won't want to go poking around in our rooms, I suppose?"

"I'm afraid we'll have to poke around everywhere in the house," Heimrich said. "And in the grounds."

"You'll be wasting your time," Ursula Jameson told him. "And suppose you do find the bow somewhere? So what?"

"We like to find weapons," Heimrich said. "Sometimes they tell us something."

"You won't find fingerprints, if that's what you're after," Ursula said. "Because people shooting arrows wear gloves. Anyway, a glove on the right hand. And a sleeve shield on the left. Everybody knows that."

Heimrich hadn't, so he said, "Mmmm." He looked at Forniss, who was standing by the fireplace. Forniss said, "Any time, Inspector. Three men outside. Waiting to poke around."

Heimrich said he might as well get them started, and Forniss said, "Yep," and went off up the long room. Heimrich said, "About the servants, Miss Jameson?"

"Over there," Ursula said, and pointed to a length of padded velvet cord which dangled from the wall be-

66

tween the double doors and the fireplace. "Just pull it, and Barnes will come."

It was, Heimrich thought, like something out of the past. The whole house was like something out of the past. He crossed to the velvet cord and pulled it.

"Do you want us to stay here?" Dr. Tennant asked. "My wife ought to be resting. So ought you, Miss Jameson."

"With policemen stamping all around?" Ursula said. "But—"

Barnes was still a thin, dark man. He was not, now, wearing a white jacket. His jacket and his trousers were dark; he wore a white shirt and a black necktie. He came in from the rear of the room and, when he was close, he said, "Miss Jameson, ma'am?"

"This policeman—" Ursula Jameson began, and the ringing of a telephone interrupted her. Barnes, without saying anything, went up the room. He took a telephone out of a small cabinet and said, "The Tor," into it. He said, "I'll see, sir." Heimrich would have somewhat expected him to say, "I shall ascertain." That would have gone better with the rest of it.

Barnes came back down the room. He said, "The call is for you, Inspector." Then he added, "Sir."

The call was from the headquarters of Troop K at the new Washington Hollow Barracks in Dutchess County. The pictures were ready. Should copies be sent down?

Heimrich said yes. Then he corrected it. "No," he said, "I'm not sure I'll be here long. Put copies on my desk. Put others in the works. Any report from the lab?"

"No prints on the arrow," the barracks told him. "Smudges. As if somebody had rubbed along it with a glove on his hand. Hollow steel. Usually shot from a heavy bow, what they say. Only, Dr. Fleming has come in with a preliminary. The wound wasn't deep. Just deep enough to kill him. Steel arrow from a heavy bow would damn well have gone right through him, they say. Come out on the other side, damn near."

"Depend on where it was shot from, naturally," Heimrich said. "Hold the pictures. I'll call in. Or come in."

He got a conventional, "Sir." He hung up, and Forniss came out of the entrance hall. He said, "Start with Jameson's office? And this room behind it?"

"Wherever you like," Heimrich said. "And do you want to take on the staff, Charlie? A hundred to one nobody'll have anything that'll help."

"Thousand to one," Forniss said. "Yep."

Heimrich raised his voice and said, "Mr. Barnes?" and Barnes came up the room to them and said, "Sir?"

"This is Lieutenant Forniss," Heimrich said. "He'd like to interview the staff. Will you get them together?"

"In here, sir?"

"Wherever'd be most convenient," Heimrich said.

"Then, sir, I'd suggest our quarters. Off the kitchen, they are."

Heimrich told him that would be fine. Barnes said, "If you'll come this way, Lieutenant?" and started toward the entrance hall. Forniss started after him, and Heimrich said, "I'm going in to Cold Harbor, Lieutenant."

Forniss said, "Sir."

Formality raises its head when in the presence of civilians. Forniss followed Barnes out of the room.

Heimrich went back down the room to the three in front of the fireplace. Dr. Tennant stood up. He held a hand down to his wife and she took it, and he pulled her up to stand beside him. Very solicitous toward her, Heimrich thought. Miss Ursula Jameson remained in her chair.

"If you've finished with us," Tennant said. "This business is a strain on my wife. A very great strain."

Ursula Jameson looked up at him. Heimrich had a suspicion that she was about to say, again, "Nonsense." She did not say anything.

"There's nothing more for now," Heimrich said. "I'll be back. I'd appreciate it if you'd all remain here in the house. And ask Mr. Rankin to stay too, for the time being. There'll be troopers in and out, I'm afraid. And Lieutenant Forniss will be here."

Tennant merely nodded his head.

"I hope," Ursula said, "that this sort of thing won't go on forever."

Heimrich said he hoped so too. He also said that, later in the day, it would be necessary for one of them—the dead man's sister or his daughter preferably—to identify the body.

"You mean," Ursula said, "that you're not sure it's my brother?"

There was a rasp in her voice again.

"No, Miss Jameson," Heimrich said. "We're quite sure, I'm afraid. But there are formalities." He paused. "Required by law," he said, and went off up the room and through the square entrance hall and out of doors to his car. Outside the sun was bright, but it was still chilly. It wasn't at all like summer any more.

He drove down the long winding drive in the tunnel of tall evergreens. Sunlight trickled between the trees onto the smooth gravel of the driveway's surface. On NY 11F Heimrich turned the Buick south toward Cold Harbor.

He did not, as he had first planned, stop in Cold Harbor to talk to Dorothy Selby and her apparently redoubtable mother. He drove on through the village toward Van Brunt. On the way he used the telephone. It rang—at least he hoped it rang—in the house of Samuel and Mary Jackson. It was not answered. Too early for them to be at church, Heimrich thought. Anyway, he

69

didn't think the Jacksons were churchgoers. He dialed again and, after some time, got the country-club manager. Yes, the Jacksons were on the course. In a foursome. Probably still on the first nine.

The ninth hole of the Van Brunt Country Club is near the clubhouse. The second nine lie beyond a road. Sure, the manager would see if he could flag Sam Jackson down as he finished the first nine.

It was a little after eleven-thirty when Heimrich reached the Van Brunt Country Club. There were already a good many cars in the parking lot. Many of the club members are ardent golfers on Sunday mornings; even on Sunday mornings when the air is crisp and there is a wind blowing.

There were half a dozen people on the terrace outside the bar. They wore sweaters; they sat with their backs to the northwest wind. Several of them were drinking coffee. One man, alone at a small table, had a glass in front of him half full of what Merton Heimrich took to be bourbon. Sam and Mary Jackson were not among the half dozen. Heimrich said, "Morning, Paul," to the man with the bourbon. Paul Stidworthy, chairman of the club's admissions committee, said, "Hi, Inspector." Heimrich went across the terrace and into the bar.

There were three men standing at the bar. As a private club, the Van Brunt Country is exempt from the New York State Law which stipulates one in the afternoon as the earliest time, on Sundays, when liquor may be sold. At least, it assumed it was, and the assumption was not challenged. The local-election district member of the state House of Representatives was one of the men at the bar. He turned from his drink as Heimrich went into the bar. He said, "Morning, M.L. What's this I hear about old man Jameson? Radio have it right?"

"Yes," Heimrich said, "I'm afraid it did, Jerry. Seen Sam Jackson around this morning?"

"Out on the course," Jerry Blankenship said. "At the eighth by now. Foursome. They let Frank and me play through on the seventh."

"That's right," the man next to Blankenship at the bar said. "Morning, Inspector."

Heimrich said, "Good morning, Mr. Bishop."

"Mixed foursome," Bishop said. "The Jacksons. Your wife, Inspector. John Alden, your nephew."

Alden is the husband of a Heimrich niece. Heimrich decided that Bishop had come close enough.

"They'll probably stop by here to warm up," Blankenship said. "It's blustery out there."

Merton Heimrich said he knew it was blustery out there. He went to a small table and sat so he could look out a window from which he could see the ninth hole. Two men and two women were walking toward it. Susan was wearing gray slacks and a red turtleneck. There was one ball on the green, and Heimrich hoped it was Susan's but doubted it would turn out to be. The bartender came from behind the bar to Heimrich's table and said, "Inspector?"

"Manage a cup of coffee, Malcolm?" Heimrich said and the bartender said he could at that, and went back to the bar.

Heimrich sipped coffee and watched the ninth hole. The ball nearest the cup was Sam Jackson's, as he had supposed it would be. He watched Jackson tap it into the cup. He watched the wind catch Susan's approach shot and carry the ball into a sand trap. He watched John Alden's shot land on the green and stop thirty feet from the hole. Mary Jackson's shot hit the green and stopped companionably close to Alden's. Heimrich finished his coffee, which he assumed had been made for a rather early breakfast for friends of members who were being put up at the club overnight, or over the weekend. He walked out of the bar and toward the ninth green. Susan got her ball, along with a good deal of sand, out of the trap. The ball hit the green and rolled toward the cup. It teetered on the edge of the cup, and Susan, slender and looking very young, used body English. The ball fell into the cup. Susan said, "Wow!" and then saw Heimrich and waved. But then an expression of anxiety came onto her thin face. She said, "Has something—" but stopped speaking because Merton was smiling at her and shaking his head.

The other three saw Heimrich then. Mary Jackson clasped both hands over her head in the gesture of acknowledged applause for victory. Alden saluted. Jackson said, "You want us, M.L.?"

"When you've finished," Heimrich said. "No hurry."

They finished. Mary Jackson holed out with one long putt. It took Alden three to make it.

They walked toward Heimrich. Susan said, "A fine invigorating morning. Do you suppose Malcolm will run to a hot buttered rum?" But then she said, "Is everything all right, dear?" and there was anxiety in her voice.

"All right," Heimrich told her. "Except for murder."

"Then it's that," Jackson said. "What Susan told us?"

Heimrich nodded his head slowly. They walked toward the clubhouse. They found a table and ordered coffee. But after a few sips, Susan stood up. She said, "I think I'll—" and looked across the table at Mary Jackson, who said, "Me too." They both stood up. Then John Alden stood. He said, "And me," and Sam Jackson and Heimrich were alone at the table.

"Tactful of them," Jackson said. "Well, M.L.?"

"Jameson was killed," Heimrich said. "Somebody shot an arrow into his neck. And I've already been told it's hard to believe. By several people."

Jackson lighted a cigarette.

72

"You were his lawyer," Heimrich said. "Also his executor, Sam?"

"No. First National of Cold Harbor."

"You drew up his will?"

"Several of them," Sam Jackson said. "Changed it several times in the last couple of years. After his second wife got herself killed, of course."

"The last one, Sam? Last night? After the party?"

"The birthday party," Sam said. "The public announcement party. Damned elaborate do, wasn't it?"

"All of that," Heimrich said. "Followed by the making of a will?"

He was told he was guessing. He said, "Naturally, Sam." He was told the relationship between counsel and client is confidential. Heimrich said, "I know that, Sam. I suppose the will was duly signed and witnessed?"

"Two of the maids," Sam Jackson said. "In the testator's presence and the presence of each other. The way the book says. All legal. Copies in my desk at home. Locked in the desk."

"Well, Sam?"

"I'll apply for probate. When that's granted, the contents will be public property."

"Meanwhile," Heimrich said, "it's murder, Sam. And you're an officer of the court."

Sam Jackson put out his cigarette. He lighted another. He looked at Heimrich through smoke. After a time he said, "All right. The hell with it."

Heimrich nodded his head and lighted himself a cigarette. He waited.

"Ten thousand to Barnes," Jackson said. "The same to the cook, Myrtle Miller. And—the same to his son. 'Who has chosen to alienate himself from the family.' He insisted on putting that in. Two hundred thousand to his daughter. Twenty-five thousand to a cousin who lives in London. Female cousin. I don't remember her name offhand. Lucinda something, I think it is. Oh yes, another ten thousand to Mr. and Mrs. Frans Frankel. 'For faithful service through the years,' like the other staff people. The house and the acreage which goes with it—he wanted it called just 'The Tor' but I got him to be more specific. 'The house known as "The Tor" and the real property appertaining thereto,' to his sister."

"No money to her, Sam?"

"She doesn't need it, apparently. Their father willed her a third of his cash assets. The rest went to the son, along with the house and land. Now she gets the house too. And maybe a couple of hundred acres. I'm just guessing on that. I've no idea as to the size of the estate. I wasn't his financial agent. Your guess is probably as good as mine. It's been a rich family for generations, and lived like a rich family. As if there weren't any bottom to the well."

"That's all of it, Sam?"

"No, M.L. 'All other property, both real and personal, of which I may die possessed' to the girl he was going to marry."

"As his wife, Sam?"

Samuel Jackson shook his head.

"As Dorothy Selby, at present a resident of Cold Harbor, New York."

"It will come to a nice round sum," Heimrich said. "A million or so, maybe?"

Sam Jackson shrugged his shoulders. He said, again, that he didn't know what it would come to. Then he said, "Whatever it comes to, she had a less drastic way of getting it. And he may not have told her how he was going to draw up his will."

"She'll be asked about that, naturally," Heimrich said.

"As to the less drastic way. Perhaps she didn't think so, Sam. Perhaps she decided that marrying a man old enough to be her father was pretty drastic."

"Her grandfather, actually," Sam Jackson said. "If everybody started reasonably early."

John Alden came back into the taproom. A few steps from the table he stopped. He said, "O.K.?"

"Sure," Heimrich said.

"It takes girls forever, sometimes," Alden said. He sat down in his chair and sipped from his cup. He shook his head and then raised it to look at Malcolm. He passed his hand over the five cups on the table and Malcolm said, "Coming right up, Mr. Alden."

"The thing is," Sam Jackson said, "they get to chatting. It's a—"

He did not finish that because Susan Heimrich and Mary Jackson came into the room and across it. It was Susan who said, "Conference all finished?"

"All finished," Heimrich said. Then he stood up. Susan said, "Oh," disappointment in her voice. "I thought maybe we could all have an early lunch. Before the other nine. As a matter of fact, instead of the other nine."

"You four, dear," Heimrich said.

Susan raised her eyebrows. Slowly, he nodded his head. Then he said, "I'm afraid so, Susan."

He left them at the table, with Malcolm bringing hot coffee. He went out to the Buick. Then he got out of the car and went back into the clubhouse, but not into the taproom. He went into a telephone booth and looked at a number he had jotted down and dialed it. The number he had dialed rang four times and he heard "The Tor." He said, "Barnes?" and got, "Barnes, sir."

"Inspector Heimrich. Lieutenant Forniss still around?"

Barnes thought so. Barnes would see. "If you'll just hold on, sir." Heimrich held on. Charles Forniss came on.

"None of the servants heard anything or saw anything," Forniss said. "Or admits hearing anything or seeing anything. However, we found the bow, all right. A bow, anyway."

Heimrich said, "Go ahead, Charlie."

They had found a bow in the closet off Jameson's office. They had also found fishing gear in the closet, and two tennis rackets, both warped out of shape, and a bag of golf clubs. Also, a pair of wading boots.

"The bow looks pretty old," Forniss said. "Not that I know anything about bows. There were also four arrows. Only there's this, M.L. They're wooden arrows."

Heimrich said, "Mmmm."

"Yeah," Forniss said. "Anyhow, I've wrapped the bow and arrows up and sent them along to the fingerprint boys. O.K.?"

"Yes," Heimrich said. "The people, Charlie?"

"Present or accounted for," Forniss said. "Rankin wanted to know if it was all right if he took a walk, and I said sure, if he didn't plan to walk too far. He's quite a boy for taking walks, isn't he?"

"Seems to be," Heimrich said. "You figure you're cleaned up there, Charlie?"

"Unless there's something else you want."

"There's a good bit else I want," Heimrich said. "But it may not be there. Suppose—" He paused to look at his watch. It was past noon. "Suppose you meet me at the Inn. We'll have a sandwich. Leave a couple of troopers there, just to be sure Mr. Rankin makes it back from his walk. O.K.?"

Forniss said, "Yeah, M.L. Take me what? About half an hour?"

76

"About that," Heimrich said, and hung up and went back to the Buick. He looked at his watch again. Twelve-fifteen. It was cold in the car; it would be warm in the club's taproom. A drink would be warming. It would be forty-five minutes before the bar opened at the Old Stone Inn. Heimrich turned on the ignition. He turned on the car heater. The air which came out of the vents was cold air. It was just beginning to be warm air when he parked the Buick at the Old Stone Inn. There were only a few other cars in the parking lot.

He locked up the Buick and walked across the parking lot. The wind was really picking up, and it was a cold wind. And yesterday it was almost still summer, Heimrich thought, and went into the taproom, which was warm but empty. The barman who had taken Harold's place was not behind the bar. But a fire was leaping in the fireplace.

Heimrich went to a corner table and sat down at it and lighted a cigarette. Maybe the girl really wanted to marry Jameson, he thought. If it keeps on like this, there'll be frost tonight. Perhaps enough to kill all Susan's marigolds and zinnias. Cold snaps don't last long this time of year. Maybe if we covered them tonight. I wonder if the girl knew about Jameson's early fishing habits? I wonder if her mother knew? I should have asked John about her. They bought their house through her.

He had finished his cigarette before the new barman appeared behind the bar. He said, "Good morning, sir." He began to polish glasses. He said, "Another fifteen minutes yet, sir." Heimrich's watch made it twenty, but it was nothing to argue about. What was this new man's name—Tom, Dick or Harry? Something like that. He said, "O.K." to Tom, Dick or Harry. He thought the expression "O.K." had become a substitute for damn near anything. He lighted another cigarette and had almost finished it when Charles Forniss, looking even bigger than usual, came into the taproom. He joined Heimrich at the table. He said it was getting damn cold outside and that Rankin had come back from his walk.

"Went down to the lake and looked at the boat and came back," Forniss said.

Tom, Dick or Harry came from behind the bar and across the taproom. He said, "Something for you, gentlemen?"

It still lacked five minutes of one by Heimrich's watch, but it was nothing to argue about. They both ordered bourbon on the rocks. Yesterday was a gin-and-tonic day, Heimrich thought.

He told Forniss what Jackson had told him about Arthur Jameson's will.

Forniss said, "Well." He said, "Think of that, now."

6

It is a short run from Van Brunt to Cold Harbor. They reached it a little after two and cruised its main street slowly. There was a store front marked, "FLORENCE SELBY, REAL ESTATE." The wording was repeated on the windows of the floor above. The door to the ground floor was a sheet of heavy plate glass. The door was locked. They looked through it into a room with several desks and two sofas.

"Looks fairly up-and-coming," Forniss said. "Not run-down any."

Heimrich agreed that Florence Selby, Real Estate, was either prosperous or making a good show of prosperity. They drove on to the Cold Harbor police station.

"No," the sergeant behind the desk told them, "they're not open Sundays usually. Except in summer. You go out Vine Street maybe a mile, and the Selby place is on the right. Got a sign like the one on the office. Want to give Mrs. Selby a ring, see if she's home?"

Heimrich did not want to give Mrs. Selby a ring. They drove a little less than a mile on Vine Street, after they had found Vine Street. The sign at the foot of a driveway was half lost in a big lilac bush, which still kept all its leaves. The sign was not exactly like the one on the office windows. The sign read: "FLORENCE SELBY, REALTOR."

Heimrich turned the Buick into the driveway and drove up it.

The drive up to the Selby house was by no means as long as that to The Tor. It climbed somewhat; it was reasonably straight except that, halfway up, it had detoured around a big maple. The Selby house was a long, low one-story, stretching across a rise. There was a turn-around in front of the long white house, and from it the driveway ran on around the house. A two-level house, Heimrich thought, with probably a garage under the rear of it. He stopped the car, and they got out and walked to the front door of the long house. Heimrich found a doorbell button and pressed it, and chimes sounded softly from inside the house.

Nothing else happened. They waited for some seconds and Heimrich pressed the button again, and the chimes sounded again. And again nobody came to the door.

"At church maybe," Forniss said. "Or some place, anyhow."

"Or," Heimrich said, "gone over to the Jameson place to offer sympathy and, as people say, anything they can do to help."

They stepped away from the door and started back toward the Buick. Trees were sighing and creaking in the wind. At the top of the big maple tree leaves were beginning to turn. They were also beginning to blow off.

"We'll wait around a—" Heimrich said, and did not finish. From somewhere there was a girl's voice. "Oh, no," the girl said, her voice clear above the grating of the blown trees.

They turned away from the car and walked the drive which circled the house. It went down steeply. When they were around the house they looked down—looked beyond a terrace to a spread of lawn.

On the lawn a slender young woman in a yellow and black pants suit and a heavier and older woman in a sweater and a tweed skirt were shooting arrows at a target. There was one arrow in the rim of the target and several others lying on the grass near it.

The older woman notched an arrow and pulled back on the bowstring and let the arrow fly. The wind caught the arrow and blew it wide of the target.

"I guess you were right, dear," the older woman said. "There's too much wind. We'll have—"

But then the two archers heard the crunch of feet on the gravel drive, and both turned.

The older woman put her bow down on the grass and walked toward Heimrich and Forniss. She was smiling. She said, "Mr. Wellingmacker! You made it after all. I'd about given you—"

"No, mother," Dorothy Selby said. "They're not your prospects." She came across the grass. "You're a police inspector, aren't you?" she said, looking up at Heimrich. "You were at Arthur's party last night?"

There was lightness in her voice and a smile in it. Her long blond hair was tossed by the wind. There was gaiety in her face and in her movements. She said, "You must think we're both crazy. Shooting arrows in a wind like this. They blow every which way, of course."

She stopped suddenly and her face changed.

"You are the policeman, aren't you?" she said.

"Heimrich. This is Lieutenant Forniss. I take it you haven't—"

"Wait a minute," the older woman said. "Heimrich? Didn't I sell a house to some relatives of yours a few years back? Down in Van Brunt? Wait a minute. Alden, that was it. John Alden. I remember because—"

"Wait, Mother," Dorothy Selby said. "Haven't what, Inspector Heimrich?"

It was, of course, quite possible, Heimrich thought. News of Arthur Jameson's death by violence had been on the radio. But not everybody listens to the radio on Sunday mornings, when radio broadcasts are apt to devote themselves to sermons and religious music. And certainly the practice of archery under the circumstances implied innocent ignorance of the circumstances. Unless the duty sergeant back in town had decided to make a telephone call on his own? Decided to alert Mrs. Florence Selby and her daughter to the impending arrival of two members of the New York State Police?

"Nobody's telephoned you today?"

Florence Selby stood with her feet apart, as if she defied not only the wind, but police asking questions. "I took my phone off the hook first thing this morning. So Dorothy could sleep. And so I wouldn't be bothered with househunters who think a real-estate agent is at their beck and call any hour of the day or night."

"Then I'm afraid I'm the one to give you bad news, Miss Selby," Heimrich said. "Very bad news, I'm sorry to say. Mr. Jameson—"

All the light went out of Dorothy Selby's young face.

"Arthur," she said. "*Something's happened to Arthur.* That's what you're going to say, isn't it?"

Her voice, which had been high and gay, was low and trembled a little. She reached out and took her mother's hand, which had reached toward her.

Heimrich has had to break bad news many times. It

82

is a policeman's lot. The response of people who hear such news is varied. Sometimes they scream and break into tears. Sometimes, with voice rising in hysteria, they fight against acceptance of the news. Now and then they faint.

And sometimes all life fades out of their faces, as light had faded out of Dorothy Selby's.

"I'm afraid Mr. Jameson is dead, Miss Selby," Heimrich said.

She said, "Oh. *Oh!*" She turned to her mother, and Mrs. Selby put her arms around the pretty young woman in the gay yellow and black pants suit. "But he was all right last night," Dorothy Selby said, her voice muffled against her mother's heavy sweater. "Last night he was all right. He—"

And then her slim body began to shake against her mother's, and she said, "No. No. *No,*" and went on saying the same word over and over in her muffled voice.

Mrs. Selby's voice did not shake. It was only a little loud. "Well, Inspector?" Florence Selby said, and her arm tightened about her daughter. "You may as well get on with it, Inspector."

"Mr. Jameson was killed this morning," Heimrich said. "Somebody shot an arrow into his neck."

The girl freed herself from her mother's arm. She turned suddenly and looked away toward the target with a single arrow stuck in the rim of it, with other arrows lying on the ground around it.

"He'd been out fishing on the lake," Heimrich said. "Apparently he was just rowing in when somebody shot him from the bank." He paused. Dorothy Selby kept on looking at the target. Then she put her hands up over her face.

It might as well be said, Heimrich decided.

"Archery isn't a very common sport around here, is it, Mrs. Selby?" he said. "Not for years, anyway. Most people play golf, or tennis."

"There're still some of us around," Mrs. Selby said. "You're sure somebody shot Mr. Jameson with an arrow?"

"Yes," Heimrich said. "With a steel arrow. Tipped with feathers."

"A steel arrow," Mrs. Selby said. "People are all the time trying to improve things. I wouldn't be caught dead with that kind of arrow. Oh! Not the best way of putting it, was that?"

"Perhaps not," Heimrich said. "Since Mr. Jameson was. Did either of you have occasion to—"

"We'll go inside," Mrs. Selby told him. "Get out of the wind if you're going to ask us questions."

She began to strip a leather glove off her right hand. On her left wrist there was a leather cuff. She saw Heimrich and Forniss watching her.

"The damn things scratch," she said. "Dig in."

The two policemen looked at Dorothy Selby, who was wearing a wrist guard but not a glove.

"The young think they know everything better," Mrs. Selby said. "Think they're tougher. Wait a minute."

She walked off across the grass and picked up her bow, and her daughter's bow, from it. She went to the target and pulled the arrow out of it. She picked up the arrows which had missed the target. She brought the bows and arrows back and held them out toward Heimrich. "Look at them," Florence Selby commanded.

Heimrich looked at them.

"All wood, aren't they?" Florence Selby said.

Heimrich agreed that the arrows, and the bows too, were wooden arrows and wooden bows.

"Come on," Mrs. Selby said, and walked off. She

marched off, Heimrich thought. She marched with no evidence of any doubt that she would be followed.

Her daughter followed her, and Heimrich and Forniss followed her. She led them toward a terrace which stretched for most of the width of the house. She led them, on the way there, past a two-car garage with two cars in it. One of the cars was a black Volks. The other was also black. It was, however, a Mercedes, and, Heimrich thought, a new one. The Mercedes is popular in that part of the country among those who can afford them.

There were director's chairs and summer chaises on the terrace and little tables by them. The wind had blown over two of the director's chairs. Well, Heimrich thought, yesterday it was summer, or almost summer. Mrs. Selby pulled open a wide sliding glass door and went through the doorway. They followed her, and Dorothy Selby, into a long room with doors at either end. Both doors stood open. At one end the door opened on a bedroom; at the other to a tiny kitchen. It was not especially warm in the long room, although it was warmer and quieter than it had been outside.

Mrs. Selby put the two bows and the half-dozen or so arrows down on a sofa. "We'll go upstairs," Mrs. Selby said. She reached back and put an arm around her daughter's shoulders. Half supporting the slighter woman, she went across the room toward a staircase. Forniss stopped and looked at the bows and arrows lying on the sofa. He looked at Heimrich. Heimrich shook his head and they followed the two women to the staircase and up it.

They went from the stairs into a large living room, comfortably furnished with deep chairs and two sofas and several tables and a large television console. There was a fieldstone fireplace at one end of the room, with a fire laid in it and not lighted. It was pleasantly warm and quiet in the big room, and sunlight came in through windows at the south end and lay on a rug which, to Heimrich's nonexpert eyes, appeared to be an Oriental.

Mrs. Selby walked firmly down the room to the fireplace, and Dorothy sank down into a deep chair. Mrs. Selby took a packet of matches from the pocket of her tweed skirt and struck one and lighted the fire. Heimrich had half expected her to use a kitchen match and strike it with her thumbnail.

Paper caught in the fireplace, and kindling caught and fire leaped up against logs—logs well laid for a fire, Heimrich thought. The fireplace was efficient; the flue drew well. Mrs. Selby was an efficient woman, except when it came to shooting arrows into a target on a windy day. Of course, it had been less windy early in the morning, and the lake below The Tor was in a sheltered place.

Mrs. Selby came back from the fireplace, and did not look behind her to see if her fire was burning well. Fires Florence Selby lighted always burned well. Mrs. Selby spoke from the middle of the room. She said, "You may as well sit down. Do you want drinks?"

Forniss shook his head and Heimrich said, "Not right now, Mrs. Selby. Just a few—"

"Well," Florence Selby said, "I do if you don't. And Dorothy needs one."

Dorothy Selby did not say anything. She sat deep in the chair, and it seemed to Merton Heimrich that she sat limply and that life had not come back into her face. Heimrich sat down in one of the less deep chairs. Forniss went down the room to the fireplace and looked into the waxing fire and then turned from it and stood leaning against the fieldstones which surrounded it. He also stood near a glass door through which Heimrich could see his Buick, its tall radio antenna waving a little in the wind.

Mrs. Selby came back from a bar at the end of the room most distant from the fireplace. She had a squat glass in either hand, one a little fuller than the other. She held the fuller glass out to her daughter, who did not at first reach for it. Mrs. Selby said, "Your drink, Dorothy," and Dorothy reached out and took the almost full old-fashioned glass.

Mrs. Selby, Heimrich thought, took her bourbon on the rocks. Dorothy got water with hers.

Florence Selby sat down, firmly, on a sofa near her daughter's chair. She took a long swallow from her glass.

"All right," she said, "did either of us have occasion to what, Inspector? Since you want to put it in that rather stilted way. Go up to The Tor this morning and shoot an arrow into Arthur Jameson? You said in his neck, didn't you?"

"In his neck," Heimrich said. "If you want it that way, Mrs. Selby, did you? Either of you?"

"You're naïve," Florence Selby said. "Do you expect we'll say yes, of course we did?"

"No," Heimrich said. "It's not often that easy, Mrs. Selby. Did either of you know that Mr. Jameson was in the habit of going fishing in early mornings? Particularly early Sunday mornings?"

"I did," Dorothy said. She had not touched her drink. She still held it in her hand. But her voice had grown somewhat stronger.

"I've worked with—for—Arthur two, three years," Dorothy said. "Taking dictation on his book. He told me about his going fishing. About how there was only one right way to cook lake bass. He told me—well, we talked sometimes. He told me a good many things, I suppose."

"That he wanted you to marry him, among other things," Heimrich said. He added, "Naturally."

"Yes."

"And you said yes," Heimrich said.

"You were at the party," Dorothy said. Her voice now was definitely stronger. There was even a kind of bite in it. Compared to her mother's voice, Dorothy's held more of a nibble than a bite, but the bite was there. "You heard what he said."

"And you were crazy," Mrs. Selby said to her daughter. "Arthur was old enough to be your grandfather."

"You've told me that, Mother," Dorothy said, and a kind of resigned quiet had come back into her voice. "You've told me that rather often, in fact."

"For all the good it did me," her mother said.

Dorothy did not answer that. She sipped from her glass.

"I take it," Heimrich said, "that you did not approve of this marriage, Mrs. Selby? Did your daughter tell you about Mr. Jameson's fishing habits?"

"Yes. I guess so. The old boy didn't have anything real to do. Never had had. People like that have to make up habits. Things they do regularly."

Heimrich said he supposed so. He said, "You went up to the Jameson house last night, Mrs. Selby. That's what we've been told, anyway. Rather late in the party. When the party was pretty much ended. To bring her home, I take it?"

"You can take it any way you like."

Mrs. Selby again drank deeply from her glass. She looked over it at Heimrich.

"Why?"

She shook her head as if the question had no meaning.

"She had stayed overnight at The Tor before," Heimrich said, and put obvious patience into his voice. "When they worked late on Mr. Jameson's book. Last night you drove up there to bring her home. But I assume she had her own car. There are two cars in your garage. A Volks and—"

"Circumstances had changed," she said. "I'd think you'd understand that. Under the new—circumstances—it wouldn't have been seemly for her to stay overnight there."

It had been years, Heimrich thought, since he had heard anyone use the word "seemly." But he nodded his head. He said, "I see, Mrs. Selby."

"Because," Mrs. Selby said, "if he felt that way about her, wanting to marry her, she shouldn't stay there overnight. It wouldn't look right. Anybody can see that, I'd think."

"You didn't approve of your daughter's marrying Mr. Jameson," Heimrich said. "You'd told her that, I gather. Merely because you thought he was too old for her?"

"Isn't that enough? Look at her, Inspector. Just look at her! She's young. She's attractive. She's got her life ahead of her. Arthur Jameson was an old man. A silly old man. In my time, we'd have called him a cradle snatcher."

Heimrich nodded his head. Jameson was also a rich old man, he thought. "Was that your only reason for opposing your daughter's marriage, Mrs. Selby?"

"I'd think that was enough. I'd seen what—" She stopped. Heimrich waited. "He was married twice before," she said. "Janet was a lot younger than he was. So is my daughter. Only more so. Both wives are dead, aren't they? Well?"

It did not seem to add to anything, in Heimrich's mind. Apparently it did add to something in Florence Selby's. He merely shook his head.

"Janet was a friend of mine," Florence said. "A very dear friend. She was hardly past her middle forties when he let her take that no-good horse. Knowing it was a no-good horse." She drank what remained in her glass. She got up and started toward the bar. She stopped midway. "Of course," she said, "she was a great one for doing what she wanted to do. Like Dorothy there. Words just bounced off of her, the way they bounce off Dorothy."

Heimrich looked at Dorothy Selby. She did not seem to be looking at anything. She lifted her shoulders slightly. She sighed. It was a sigh of resignation.

"Miss Selby," Heimrich said, "did you know—"

Mrs. Selby turned from the bar. She said, "Just wait until I come back, will you? Before you start to bully the girl?"

The tone was one of command. Heimrich said, "Certainly, Mrs. Selby." He lighted a cigarette, and made his waiting evident. Mrs. Selby came back, carrying a glass of bourbon on ice. She sat down where she had sat before. She said, "All right. Did she know what?"

"That last night after the party," Heimrich said, "Mr. Jameson drew up a new will—or signed a new will, anyway. In it, I understand, Miss Selby is his residual legatee. Which means—"

"I know what it means," Mrs. Selby said. "You think I'm illiterate? Not to Ursula?"

"To Miss Selby," Heimrich said. "Miss Jameson gets the house and land. From what I understand, Miss Jameson is already a rich woman. Miss Selby, did you know about this bequest? It's not, as I get it, contingent on your marrying him. I mean, there are no strings attached."

Dorothy Selby looked at him. She lifted her glass and drank from it.

"Well, girl?" Mrs. Selby said.

Still the girl hesitated. Mrs. Selby said, "Well?" again, in a sharper tone. She said, "Wake up, Dorothy!"

"He said something about it," Dorothy said, her voice low and the words coming slowly. "I asked him not to. I asked him to wait, anyway, until we were married. I—I thought he had agreed to. You say he actually signed a will saying that?"

"Yes," Heimrich said. "He'd signed a will saying that. Last night. After your mother had—had taken you home. You did take her home, Mrs. Selby?"

"She's got her own car. She drove back in it. I followed her in mine. She—"

Dorothy interrupted her mother. She said, "You think I killed him, don't you, Inspector? To get all that money. That's what you think, isn't it?"

"Now, Miss Selby," Heimrich said, "I don't think anything yet."

Which was truer than he liked to admit to himself.

"Because," the girl said, "I'm going to get a lot of money now that he's dead. Because you saw me using a bow and arrow."

"That's nonsense, girl," her mother said, and spoke sharply. "The man's not a fool. Anyway, you're not very good at it. Not half as good as I am, for all you're so much younger. And anyway, you were here all morning." She turned to Heimrich. "I can tell you that, Inspector. That Volks of hers makes a lot of noise when it starts up. She'd have had to go right under my windows. And—I was awake at about six. At a few minutes after six, actually. The—I guess it was the wind woke me up. Or—"

Heimrich waited.

"All right," she said. "I was worried about the girl. I couldn't sleep. That was it."

Dorothy said, "Oh, Mother."

"I'd have heard you," Mrs. Selby said. "You ought to do something about that car, Dorothy. It sounds as if it were falling apart."

"It's just a little noisy," Dorothy said. "It's perfectly all right."

"Tomorrow," Mrs. Selby said, "we're going to buy you a new one. I won't have you rattling around in that wreck any more."

Dorothy said, "Oh, *Mother*," in a voice heavy with resignation.

Heimrich stood up. He said, "We'll be getting along now, Mrs. Selby."

"That's all you're going to ask us?"

"For now," Heimrich said, "that's all we're going to ask you, Mrs. Selby. You both say you didn't drive up to Jameson's place this morning and shoot an arrow into him."

"Did you expect us to say anything else, Inspector?"

"No," Heimrich said. "I wouldn't have expected either of you to say anything else."

"I suppose you're going to confiscate our bows and arrows?"

Heimrich shook his head. He thought the expression on Florence Selby's face was one of some disappointment. He walked up the room, and Lieutenant Forniss opened the door for him. He turned in the doorway. "You can tell if a gun has been used recently, Mrs. Selby," he said. "I don't see how you could tell about a bow."

When they were in the Buick, Charles Forniss said, "Phew."

"Yes," Heimrich said, "Mrs. Selby is quite somebody, Charlie. Probably bullies a lot of people into buying houses they don't really want to buy."

He turned the radio on, tuned to the State Police frequency. It began to babble at them.

"At a percentage," Charles Forniss said. "She's in a

92

pretty good line of business, at a guess. The place looks like it."

Heimrich guided the Buick down the driveway. He said, "No, I don't think they're much in need of money, Charlie. But it's hard to guess what people think they need, naturally. I wonder if the girl's Volks does make all that racket."

"Some of them do," Charlie said and reached out for the radio transmitter because, out of the jumble of cross talk the words, "Car Ten. Car One-oh. Acknowledge, please."

Charles Forniss said, "Car Ten."

"Inspector Heimrich to call in, please. Inspector Heimrich to—"

"Message received," Forniss said. "Over and out."

They went in search of a telephone which would not jangle with static. They went to the Cold Harbor police station, and Heimrich went into it. He was gone several minutes, and when he came out to the car he came shaking his head.

"Apparently," he said, when he was back under the wheel, "the bow you found wasn't the one we want, Charlie. One of the lab boys—one who knows a little about archery, apparently—thought it looked pretty old. Pretty beat up was the way he put it. Tried pulling the bowstring. Pulled it, he says, only a couple of inches before it broke."

Forniss said, "Mmmm."

"Yes," Heimrich said, "according to the lab boy it belongs in a museum. If it belongs anywhere."

Forniss said, "Mmmm," again. Then he said, "Seems to me I read somewhere that they sometimes make bows out of steel. Ever hear of that, M.L.?"

"Until today," Heimrich said, "I can't remember hearing much of anything about bows. Steel, you say? The bottom of the lake, Charlie?"

Charles Forniss said it could be.

"You waded out to the boat," Heimrich said. "You and Mr. Rankin. I gather it isn't a very deep lake?"

"Not as far as I went," Forniss said. "Only, it was shelving down. Could be it's a lot deeper twenty-thirty feet out."

"The bottom, Charlie?"

"Felt soft," Forniss said. "Squushy." He paused and lighted a cigarette. "Yep," he said. "A steel bow probably would sink into it, M.L. If somebody stood on the bank and threw it. You could hurl a steel bow quite a distance, I'd think. If you held onto one end of it and swung." He paused again. "If you were strong enough," he said. "This gardener guy, Frankel his name is, is pretty hefty. So is Rankin, come to that. But so's this cook of theirs."

"And," Heimrich said, "it wouldn't take a hell of a lot of strength. Just a good swing. I suppose we'll have to drag."

"A steel-rod sort of thing," Forniss said, and stubbed out his half-smoked cigarette in the ashtray. "With a string tied to both ends of it. In the mud. Maybe under the mud, if it hit that way."

"Yes," Heimrich said, "we'll need luck, Charlie. And if we get it, what'll we get? A steel-rod sort of thing with a string tied to it. You saw that Mrs. Selby was wearing a glove. Maybe they all wear gloves when they're shooting arrows at targets. Or at people, naturally."

"The girl wasn't wearing a glove," Forniss said. "Not when we saw her." He shook his head. "If somebody had to kill the old boy," he said, "why didn't he use a gun? A bow and arrow, for God's sake!"

94

"Guns make a lot of noise," Heimrich said. "And also maybe a gun wasn't as handy—"

"Car Ten," came out of the radio's mumble. "Car One-oh. Come in, Car Ten."

Forniss said, "Car Ten, go ahead," into the transmitter. "Message for—"

And then static took over, blared over words. Forniss turned the radio up. The static went into a roar. He said, "Damn the God-damn thing."

"Thunderstorm around probably," Heimrich said. "We've had the wind shift."

They had been cruising up NY 11F, toward The Tor. Heimrich pulled the Buick to the side of the road. He got out of it and Forniss slid across into the driver's seat. Heimrich went into the rear of the car and pulled the telephone out of the box it lived in. He got the operator, and static. He got the Washington Hollow Barracks. He said, "Inspector Heimrich. You have a message for me? The radio's conked out."

He got a renewed blast of static for an answer. There were a few words mixed with the jagged rush of sound. He said, "I can't read you. Try—"

Suddenly, the static faded out. A voice came through, and the words came through. Heimrich listened to the words. He said, "All right, we're on our way." He hung up and went back to the front seat and sat beside Charles Forniss.

"Dr. Tennant has fallen downstairs," Heimrich said. "The stairs down to the lake. He seems to have landed on his head."

7

There were two State Police cruisers in front of the big fieldstone house on top of the hill—on top of the tor. One of them was empty. There was a trooper in the other, and the radio was chattering in a monotone. The static seemed to have gone out of this radio. When Heimrich pulled the Buick alongside the talkative car, the trooper got out of it and saluted and said, "Sir." Heimrich said, "Dr. Tennant?"

"On the way to the hospital, Inspector," the trooper said. "Pretty well banged up, the man in the ambulance said. Not conscious when they brought him up. Up those stairs he fell down. Had some trouble getting him up, sir."

Probably, Heimrich thought, it was the same ambulance which had taken the body of Arthur Jameson to the mortuary of the Cold Harbor hospital. Probably the attendants were getting used to carrying bodies up the steep staircase.

"The others?" Heimrich said. "The family?"

"Mrs. Tennant went with her husband in the ambulance. The rest of them are in the house, I guess. Corporal Purvis is with them. That's Corporal Asa Purvis, Inspector. He—well, he thought you'd maybe want to talk to them about this accident. Coming on top of the other thing, the way it did. Want I should show you where it happened, sir?"

"The stairs down to the lake, wasn't it?" Heimrich said.

"Yes, sir," the trooper said. "Damn steep stairs. Only there's a railing down them."

Heimrich told the trooper that they knew the stairs. He and Forniss went to the head of the steep flight of brick stairs. There was another trooper at the bottom of them. He was sitting on a stone outcropping and smoking a cigarette. When he saw Heimrich and Forniss he stood up and ground his cigarette out on the grass. Then he called up to them. He called, "Watch it, Inspector. They're damn tricky."

Heimrich had been down and up the stairs. He knew they were steep and tricky and led a long way down. As he had earlier, he used the support of the iron railing which went down along the staircase, which had narrow treads. The bricks of the staircase were old, and some of them had crumbled a little with the years. On the third tread down, one of the bricks moved a little under Heimrich's foot. Heimrich clutched the iron rail and went on, and Forniss, also sliding a hand down the rail, went after him. It occurred to Heimrich that the stairs were even trickier than they had been that morning. He thought that, he supposed, because a man had recently fallen down them.

He was about a quarter of the way down the flight of stairs when he stopped. One section of the iron rail had been pulled loose from its stanchion and jutted inward for some inches over the stairs. Heimrich leaned down and looked at the broken rail. The end which had parted from the upright holding it was deeply rusted. It had, evidently, rusted almost through. It had seemed solid enough a few hours before. A few hours before, Heimrich did not remember that he had put much weight on it. He had merely used the rail for guidance.

He said, "Watch it, Charlie," over his shoulder and went on down the stairs. He still kept a hand on the rail, but he kept it there with little confidence. He got to the bottom of the stairs. There was dried blood on the bottom steps and on the path beyond them. There were footprints in the blood on the stairs.

Heimrich managed to avoid stepping in the dried blood. He looked back up the flight of stairs. It was a long way to fall. He turned to the trooper.

"Asa told me to come down here, Inspector," the trooper said. "Said to keep an eye on things. That's Asa Purvis, sir. He's a corporal. Said just to keep an eye on things."

"Yes," Heimrich said. "Who found Dr. Tennant, you happen to know?"

"His wife, seems like. Way I hear it, he'd gone out for a walk, and she thought he was gone a long time and went looking for him. Went to the top of the stairs and looked down and saw him. I was sitting in the car up there—" He gestured up there. "Along with Ben. He's my sidekick. And she let out a yell and I ran over and there he was. Sort of crumpled up, like. So Ben sort of helped her get back in the house and called in for the ambulance, and I went—came—on down here. She was screaming a lot and tried to come down with me, but we thought—well, that maybe she'd better not.

On account of from up there he looked pretty bashed up and maybe dead. Only when I got down, he was still breathing, and then Asa came down with first-aid stuff and we tied him up, sort of. He was still bleeding. That's pretty much the way it was, Inspector. We did everything we could, I guess."

"I'd think so," Heimrich said. "Ambulance long in getting here?"

"Maybe twenty minutes, sir. Maybe half an hour. We'd pretty much got the bleeding stopped."

"When you came down," Heimrich said. "That section of the rail up there. Pretty much as it is now?"

"Out farther, Inspector. Stretched—oh, about half-way across the steps. They had to bend it back to get the stretcher up."

"Dr. Tennant was unconscious when you got down to him?"

"He sure was. Out like—" The trooper hesitated momentarily and realized he had already trapped himself. "Like a light." He seemed about to go on. Heimrich said, "Yes?"

"Way I see it," the trooper said, "he was holding onto the rail and it gave way and he lost his balance. Funny thing, place like this they'd let a rail rust out that way."

"Probably never noticed it," Heimrich said. "Apparently rusted out where it went through the stanchion. Not in sight unless you looked carefully. Or, naturally, pulled on it hard."

The trooper said it could have been that way, sir, he guessed.

Heimrich looked at the bottom steps and at the path beyond them. Tennant had bled a good deal. But scalp wounds bleed freely. There was nothing further to be done there. They went back up the stairs, past the broken rail which jutted toward them, and into the house. It was Asa Purvis, Corporal, New York State Police, who opened the door for them. He said, "Inspector. Lieutenant." There was something almost of awe in his voice when he said, "Inspector." It was, after all, Inspector M. L. Heimrich who had helped him get into the State Police.

Heimrich said, "Hello, Asa," and went to find a telephone other than the one in the drawing room. There was one at the back of the square entrance hall.

Dr. James Tennant was in surgery. The extent of his injuries had not been determined. They apparently included a fractured skull. He had not regained consciousness and in any case was anesthetized. It was too early for a prognosis. Brain damage was possible; it was, indeed, likely.

Mrs. James Tennant had been given a room in the hospital. She was under mild sedation, against which she had protested.

"I'll be at the Jameson place for a while," Heimrich said. "If there's any change in the doctor's condition, let me know, will you?"

The hospital would. Heimrich made a second call. Washington Hollow Barracks would get technical men down.

Heimrich and Forniss went into the long drawing room of The Tor. Asa Purvis was standing near the door. Miss Ursula Jameson and her nephew and Geoffrey Rankin were sitting in front of the fire, which had been let burn down. Miss Jameson, still in black sweater and black slacks, had a coffee cup on the table in front of her. She was sitting on the sofa which faced the fire, and Ronald Jameson was sitting beside her. He had a glass in his hand. Rankin, also with a glass, was in a chair at the end of the sofa. He got up as the two big policemen came down the room.

Ursula Jameson lifted her coffee cup. Then she put it down again in the saucer; clicked it down into the saucer.

"This is a bad day," Ursula said. "A terrible day. You were on the phone out there. Calling the hospital?"

"Yes, Miss Jameson."

She lifted the coffee cup again and put it down again. She said, "Well, Inspector?"

"He's in surgery," Heimrich said. "They don't know yet, they say. Probably a fractured skull. He's unconscious."

"Somebody said the railing broke," the woman in black sweater and black slacks said. "Was that what happened?"

"It seems to have been," Heimrich said. He pulled a chair up near Rankin's. Forniss leaned against the fireplace stones.

"I kept telling Arthur he ought to have something done," Ursula said. "Over and over I told him. Finally he listened. Anyway, he said somebody was coming tomorrow to check on it. He never used it himself. He—he wouldn't admit to needing it. So many things he wouldn't—" She did not finish.

"You're talking about the railing, Miss Jameson?"

"Of course. Frankel told me about it and I told Arthur. Kept telling him. Told him it was dangerous. And now look."

"Yes," Heimrich said. "You say Frankel told you the rail was rusting. You hadn't noticed it yourself?"

"It's been years since I went down those stairs. Years and years. I knew when I was getting too old for that sort of thing. Arthur would never—" She stopped and

101

shook her head. She lifted her coffee cup again and this time drank from it.

"Suppose one of you tells me what happened," Heimrich said. He looked at Ursula Jameson, but she merely looked into the fire. Heimrich doubted whether she really saw the fire she looked at.

"We had lunch," Ronald Jameson said. "A drink or two and then lunch. All of us. Right here. Sandwiches. That sort of thing. We—well, none of us was very hungry."

"Naturally," Heimrich said. "You, Mr. Jameson, and your aunt and Dr. and Mrs. Tennant. And Mr. Rankin. All of you."

"You told me to stay," Rankin said. "I don't know why. That's what you told me."

"Asked you," Heimrich said. "Yes. You had drinks and sandwiches here in front of the fire. About when was that, Mr. Jameson?"

"Finished about two. Somewhere around then."

"And?"

Ursula Jameson looked away from the fire. She looked at Heimrich.

"I went out on the terrace for a minute or two. To get a little air. Then I went upstairs to lie down," she said. "I took one of those pills Jim Tennant had been trying to get me to take. I think that I dozed off a little. And then Ron came up to tell me—to tell me what had happened. What else had happened."

"The rest of you?"

"What difference does it make?" Jameson said.

Heimrich said he didn't know what difference it made.

"Well," Jameson said, "I was out of cigarettes. Drove into town to get a carton. Took a while to find a place open. Close up tight on Sundays, these little places do.

102

When I got back, there didn't seem to be anybody around. I went on up to my room."

Heimrich said he saw. He said, "You, Mr. Rankin?"

"Jim and Estelle and I sat here for a while," Rankin said. "Just—oh, sort of sat around. Then Estelle said she was going up and lie down, and Jim said something about that being a good idea, and that he was going to get a little air and then he'd be up."

"Suggest that you come with him?"

"No. Just went out through one of the doors over there. Estelle went upstairs, and after a while I did too. I'd brought some papers out I thought I might as well go over. And, if you want to know, Inspector, I felt like that fifth wheel they talk about."

"Mrs. Tennant apparently went out later," Heimrich said. "Looking for her husband, does any of you know?"

"I suppose it was that way," Ronald Jameson said. Nobody else said anything. "First thing I knew, I heard Stel screaming. I had a window open, and my room's on that side of the house. So I ran downstairs and—one of the troopers had got there first. He was holding onto her and she kept on screaming. They were at the top of those damned stairs and I—well, I looked down and could see what was making her scream. So I said something like I'd take her, and the trooper went down the stairs. She was shaking and I kept saying silly things like he'd be all right and she kept on screaming. But then she sort of—well, sagged, and I thought she was going to faint and brought her in here."

"About when was this, Mr. Jameson?"

Jameson did not know exactly. He thought perhaps about three. He had got his half sister into the drawing room and in front of the fire. "She just sort of sat there shaking." He had rung for Barnes and got him and one of the maids. Barnes and the maid had stayed with Estelle Tennant while he went upstairs and told his aunt what had happened.

"I guess I woke you up, Aunt Ursula," Jameson said.

She seemed to come back from a long way off. She said, "What?" in a dazed voice and her nephew repeated what he had said.

"I wasn't really asleep," Ursula said. "Not really."

They waited for her to go on. She went back to looking toward the fire.

"When I came down," Ronald Jameson said, "one of the troopers was on the telephone. Calling an ambulance. And then somewhere else. I know he said, 'Better try to get onto him.' That would have been you, I guess, Inspector?"

"Yes. And you?"

"Went in to see how Sis was making out. Because she kept saying, 'I've got to go. I've got to go to him.' She sounded—well, pretty hysterical. They'd only been married a few years, you know."

"Three years," Ursula Jameson said, speaking to the fire. "Three years last May. He'd been married before, of course."

Heimrich waited for her to go on. She did not go on. He looked at Jameson.

"The maid was holding onto her," Jameson said. "Barnes was saying, 'You'd better not, Mrs. Tennant. You'd better not. He'll be all right.' So I went in and held onto her and said—hell, I guess I wasn't any better at saying anything. She kept trying to get up and I kept holding her. And after what seemed like one hell of a time the ambulance came. I told the maid to keep her there and went to the door and they—they were bringing him up on a stretcher. And then I heard Sis say, 'Let me go, damn you,' very loudly and then she ran up the room to the door and said, 'I'm going with him. You can't stop me!' So—well, I didn't try to stop her. Maybe I should have."

"No," Heimrich said. "Anyway, she found out he was still alive. And went with him. Miss Jameson?"

She turned slowly from the fire. She said, "What?"

"You came downstairs?"

"After a while," she said. "When I first—first got up I was dizzy. That pill, I suppose. I was halfway down the stairs when I saw her run out the door and get into the ambulance. Then Ron said something like, 'I couldn't stop her,' and helped me in here. I was still a little dizzy. Dazed, I guess you'd call it."

"Mr. Rankin?"

"They put me in a room on the other side of the house," Rankin said. "I didn't hear anything until I heard the ambulance. The siren, I mean. I didn't pay much attention. You're always hearing sirens. But I opened my door and heard people talking, so I came down. The ambulance was just going down the drive. And then somebody—it was you, wasn't it, Jameson?— told me what had happened."

Heimrich nodded his head. He said he thought he had got it clear enough. He stood up and started up the long room, and Forniss went after him.

"They'll be along pretty soon," Heimrich told Forniss at the door. "The railing, of course. And anything you can get out of the staff."

Forniss said, "Yep." He watched Heimrich go out to the Buick. He didn't need to be told where Heimrich was going.

The surgical resident at the Cold Harbor Memorial Hospital said, "We've done what we can, Inspector. He's in Intensive Care. It's too early to tell."

"His chances?"

The surgeon shrugged and spread his hands. Heimrich waited.

"Critical," the surgeon said. "Fracture and some brain damage. Oh, he's got a fair chance to live. But—" Again he shrugged and spread his hands.

"We can't tell yet," he said. "Thing now is to keep him alive. We're trying. There's a neurologist—neurological surgeon—they know. We've got in touch with him and he's coming up tonight. He's a good man. One of the best in this part of the country. If anybody—" Once more he shrugged his shoulders. "Dr. Tennant is a neurologist himself, his wife says. Did you know that?"

"I'd heard he was a psychiatrist," Heimrich said, and the resident said, "Both."

"He hasn't regained consciousness?"

"No. Just stayed alive. Which was a lot, under the circumstances."

"Assuming he recovers, Doctor, will he remember what happened? Remember falling? Why he decided to go down that flight of stairs?"

"Perhaps. Eventually. I keep telling you, just now the thing is to keep him alive. As to his ever remembering much about the accident, my guess would be he won't. It may—well, it may be a long time before he remembers who he is. But that's just a guess. I'm a general surgeon, not a specialist. Dr. Wenning—he's the man from New York who's coming up—may be able to make an evaluation. You'll just have to wait, Inspector. You're interested because of Jameson, I suppose? The cadaver downstairs?"

"That enters in, naturally," Heimrich said. "Mrs. Tennant?"

"She was hysterical when they came in," the doctor said. "We've—well, we've calmed her down some. Put her in a room with a special nurse to—well, to hold her

106

hand is what it amounts to. Do what she can. After all, the injured man's a doctor too. I won't say that makes a difference, but—"

He was a great man to shrug his shoulders, Heimrich thought.

Whether he could see Mrs. Tennant would pretty much be up to the floor nurse. And the doctor on the floor, of course. And it was quite possible that Mrs. Tennant would be asleep. Which would, obviously, be the best thing for her. Still—

"Third floor," the doctor said. "They'll tell you what room. And if she's sleeping they'll want you to wait until she wakes up. Elevator's over there."

Heimrich went to the elevator. He waited while an elderly woman was wheeled out of it. A much younger woman was walking beside the chair. The younger woman said, "Yes, Mother. You're really going home now." Heimrich got into the elevator and pressed the button numbered "3."

The nurse in charge of the floor said that Mrs. Tennant was having no visitors. Mrs. Tennant was in shock. Also, she was under sedation. It would be much better if—

Heimrich told her who he was. He said it was important. He said he wouldn't stay long. The nurse said, "Well, I'll see. If she's awake—"

She used the telephone and on it her voice was very low. She put the telephone back. She said, "Nurse Cunningham thinks that it will be all right for just a few minutes. But you'll have to remember that Mrs. Tennant is in shock, Inspector."

Heimrich promised to remember. He walked along a corridor to Room 323. The door was closed. A nurse opened it when he knocked, very gently. "She's awake," the nurse said. "A little groggy from the medication.

107

You must try not to upset her." Heimrich promised he would try not to upset Estelle Tennant.

Her black hair was still smooth against the pillow. Her brown eyes looked even larger than they had when he had first seen her. When he first stood at the foot of the bed and looked down at her, he thought there was almost no expression in her eyes. But then expression came into them.

"You're that police officer," Estelle said. Her voice was very low and it shook a little. But then she tried to sit up in the hospital bed. The nurse said, "There, dear. Just—" and went to her, but Estelle Tennant ignored the nurse.

"You've come to tell me something," Estelle said and her voice went up. "That's it, isn't it? *That Jim's—*"

"No," Heimrich said. "There's been no change in your husband's condition, Mrs. Tennant. No change for the worse. I'm just trying to find out what happened. Do you feel up—"

He broke off because she had lain back against the pillows and closed her strangely large eyes.

"He fell down those stairs," Estelle Tennant said. "Those dreadful stairs. Why did he always go that way? Down those stairs, I mean?"

"I don't know," Heimrich said. He pulled a light chair up beside the bed and sat down on it. "It's one of the things I've been wondering about, Mrs. Tennant. Thought perhaps you might be able to tell me, if you're up to it. If it'll be too much—"

"He went out for a walk after lunch," she said. She opened her eyes and her voice seemed a little stronger, a little more certain. "He almost always does. After lunch. Between appointments. Even in the city. It's—it's just one of his habits."

108

"He went today," Heimrich said. "And you went up to your room."

"I thought perhaps I could sleep. And—and forget what had—forget about Father. But I couldn't, of course. I—I kept remembering."

"Yes," Heimrich said. He waited.

"I expected Jim to come back," she said. "I kept waiting. I thought—I thought he ought to know I needed him. But he didn't come. He just didn't come. And all the time—"

She closed her eyes and put her hands over them. Her body began to tremble in the bed.

"I think," the nurse said, "that Mrs. Tennant has had—"

But the girl in the bed took her hands away from her face and opened her eyes. She said, "No, nurse. I'm all right. After a while, Inspector, I—I couldn't wait any longer. I couldn't wait there alone any longer. So I went out—to try to find him."

She shuddered again, but only for an instant. She said, "I'm all right, nurse."

"You went to the top of this flight of stairs," Heimrich said. "Why did you go there, Mrs. Tennant? Had your husband said anything about going down to the lake?"

"He usually went that way," Estelle said. "I suppose that's why I went there first. And—and looked down the stairs and—"

She moved her head back and forth against the pillow and again her slender body trembled under the light covering. The nurse said, "Inspector. I must—" but again Estelle said, "No, nurse," and this time her voice was almost sharp.

"When he left you and the others," Heimrich said.

"To go out for a walk. Were you surprised, Mrs. Tennant?"

"No. Why should I have been surprised? I just told you he often went for walks. Almost every day."

"He just stood up and said he thought he'd go out for a little air? Something like that, as you remember it?"

"Yes. He looked at his watch and said—pretty much what you just said. That he thought he'd get a breath of air. Something like that. And I said—oh, asked him not to be too long. Said I thought I'd go up and lie down. He went through one of the french doors and out onto the terrace. If you're going down to the lake you go that way."

Heimrich nodded his head. She looked at him and her eyes were very wide.

"You say he looked at his watch before he went out of the room," Heimrich said. "As if—oh, as if he wanted to be some place at a certain time? As if, perhaps, he had an appointment at a certain time?"

"I didn't think that then," she said. "He runs on a schedule, of course. I mean, patients are due at certain hours and he has to keep track. But up here—well, time doesn't matter so much, of course."

"But this afternoon he did look at his watch. And you remember he did. Why, do you think?"

"I don't know why he did," Estelle Tennant said. "Just—oh, everybody now and then wonders what time it is."

"I didn't mean precisely that," Heimrich said. "What I wondered was why you remember Dr. Tennant's looking at his watch. Sometimes we remember things because they surprise us. Thinking back now, do you think that you remember your husband's looking at his watch because you were surprised he did?"

She closed her eyes for a moment. Then she opened

them and shook her head. Her head moved very slowly.

"I don't think so," she said. "At least, I don't remember being surprised. Of course, I may have wondered a little, I suppose. Because—well, because we weren't going any place. At any special time, I mean. But I don't know why I remembered anything so—so unimportant as Jim's looking at his watch." She shook her head again, slowly against the pillow.

Then, abruptly, she sat up in bed.

"What do they tell you about Jim?" she said, and her voice was high. "Only I suppose you won't tell me, will you? Nobody will tell me, will they?" There was shrillness in the voice which had been so soft, so almost hesitant.

"They've finished surgery, Mrs. Tennant. Your husband is in the—what they call the recovery room, I think. He's still unconscious, of course. Still under the anesthetic. There's no reason not to—not to be hopeful, Mrs. Tennant. And there's another doctor coming up from—"

"I know," she said. "I told them about Frank. Frank Wenning. He's a very famous doctor. He and Jim interned together. They're old friends, you see. Frank went in for surgery. He's really coming?"

"Yes. They say he's on his way."

"If anybody—" she said, and moved her head again, but this time nodded it, as if she were affirming something to herself. Then she said, "How did Jim come to fall, Inspector? What made him fall?"

"We don't know," Heimrich said. "He may have put too much weight on the railing that goes down beside the stairs and it gave way and he lost his balance. One section of the railing does seem to have given away. Rusted away, apparently."

"It's been there a long time, that railing," Estelle said. "Since I was a little girl. I wasn't supposed to go

111

down those stairs when I was a little girl. Aunt Ursula always said they were dangerous. I—"

Suddenly she covered her eyes with her hands again and now she began to sob.

"All right, Inspector," the nurse said. This time there was command in her voice. And this time Estelle Tennant did not say, "No, nurse!"

Heimrich went out of the room and down in the elevator and out to the parked Buick. He thought about a watch, and that people most often look at their watches when they have appointments to keep.

8

"On the rail," Lieutenant Forniss said, "plenty of prints. Mostly smeared. People slide their hands down a rail like that. A few clear ones here and there. Yours and mine, at a guess. They'll check when they get back to the barracks. Dr. Tennant's on the first section. Seem to match prints from the room he and his wife have here. Quite clear, his prints. Almost as if he had held onto the rail by his fingertips. Farther down, Rankin's. Again matching prints in his room. But we know he went down there. A few which probably are the troopers'. And a lot of smudges."

Merton Heimrich has known Charles Forniss for a good many years. He can make guesses about him. Now he guessed that Forniss was leading up to something.

"The thing is," Forniss said, "there's nothing at all on the section of the rail that pulled loose. Oh, a smudge where somebody pushed it back out of the way before they brought the doctor up on the stretcher. But on the other side—the outboard side if you know what I mean—nothing at all. Not even a smudge."

"As if somebody had wiped it off, Charlie? After somebody had pulled it loose? Or loosened it enough so it would come loose when weight was put on it?"

"Yep," Forniss said. "Could be like that, M.L. I've got a couple of men coming up to drag the lake. For what good it will do. Simpler if they use Jameson's boat. On account of it's the only boat on the lake. O.K.?"

"Yes, Charlie. I don't think the boat's going to tell us anything. They got Mr. Jameson's fish out of it, I suppose?"

"Yep. This man Frankel got them out. The gardener. Handyman. Whatever." Heimrich nodded his head. "Says he buried them. Thought at first he'd have his wife cook them and decided not to. He says, 'It wouldn't have seemed right, somehow. Way things are.' "

"I can see his point," Heimrich said. "The others? After I left?"

"Miss Jameson went back upstairs," Forniss said. "Said she thought she'd lie down. Jameson and this man Rankin each had another drink. Then Jameson went upstairs. Rankin just—oh, sort of walked around. Looked out of windows. Restless, sort of. He wants to know why the hell he can't get on back to New York."

"He asked you that?"

"He sure as hell did. Said we didn't have any legal right to make him stay here. I said we weren't making him. That we'd just rather he did. He wanted to know why. Why the hell?"

"What did you tell him, Charlie?"

"That it was up to you, M.L. That you had your reasons. Incidentally, what are your reasons? He just happened to be here, way I get it. Invited to this party last night. Had a few too many, maybe, and Jameson asked him to stay over. So with him I sort of played it dumb." He paused and looked at Heimrich and raised his eyebrows. "Of course," Forniss said, "could be I am."

"He came up with Dorothy Selby," Heimrich said. "At least, he stopped by the Selby house and she guided him up. In the Volks, I suppose. He's got a car here?"

"Chrysler," Forniss said. "Chrysler Imperial. This Miss Selby? She's quite a looker, isn't she?"

"Yes, she is," Heimrich said. "I think Rankin thinks she's quite a looker, too. And she was going to marry Jameson."

Forniss said, "Yep."

"Yes," Heimrich said. "Susan and I saw them together last night at the party. Rankin and Miss Selby. They seemed—well, they seemed to enjoy being together, Charlie. And Rankin himself suggested that perhaps I thought he'd killed Jameson. You heard him, Charlie."

"Yep," Forniss said. "And he used to shoot arrows when he was a kid. Also, he says he didn't know about last night's being an engagement party. Could be he's lying, of course. Thing is, did he bring a bow and arrow along on the off chance? Conspicuous thing to carry around, a bow. No luggage in his room, since he didn't plan to stay over. Of course, the Imperial's a big car. Plenty of trunk space. Still—you think he and Miss Selby were that way about each other, M.L.?"

"I thought so last night," Heimrich said. "He about her, anyway. Sometimes you can tell. Or think you can tell, naturally. Could have been a bit of a shock when Jameson announced Dorothy was going to marry him."

"So he went around looking for a bow and arrow, M.L.? Doing it the hard way, I'd think. Why not just use his hands? He's a husky type. Jameson wasn't."

115

Heimrich shrugged his shoulders. He thought he had perhaps picked up a habit from watching the resident surgeon at the Cold Harbor Hospital.

"O.K.," Forniss said, "You're the doctor."

It was a routine cliché. But it stuck oddly in Merton Heimrich's mind. He'd been thinking of a doctor who shrugged his shoulders a lot. He thought of another doctor—a doctor who was a psychiatrist.

"A few years ago," Heimrich said, and spoke as much to himself as to Charles Forniss, "I was watching some men playing tennis at the club. Sitting on the grass beside a doctor who's a member. A psychiatrist, like Dr. Tennant. And, apropos of nothing I could get, this doctor said, 'He's an epileptic. The one who's serving now.' Like that, out of a clear sky. Nothing I could see about his movements that showed anything. The guy who was serving was just a kid, and far's I could see, an active, healthy kid."

He stopped speaking and, after a moment or two, Forniss said, "So, M.L.?"

"The kid came up for induction a few months later," Heimrich said. "He was rejected because of epilepsy. Oh, minor. What they call petit mal. Fully controlled, as long as he took his medication. But not for the Army."

"You mean," Forniss said, "just from watching him play tennis?"

"The doctor was a new member," Heimrich said. "Didn't know the kid or his family. Doesn't practice in Van Brunt. Yes, Charlie, just from looking at him, far as I know. I asked him, later. The doctor, I mean. He said that any trained man could tell."

Forniss waited.

"Dr. Tennant is a trained man," Heimrich said. "A psychiatrist and, as it turns out, a neurologist too. Per-

116

haps things you and I wouldn't notice are giveaways to him."

"And got half killed because of something he noticed? It's a damn uncertain way of killing anybody, M.L. Loosening a handrail so he'll fall downstairs."

"Yes," Heimrich said. "And it's turned out that way. So far, at any rate. But shooting an arrow at somebody isn't a very certain way either, Charlie."

"Armies used to use them."

"A long time ago," Heimrich said. "Methods have—improved, I suppose they call it. Enough so you can wipe out a planet, not a single man. Probably just what we'll do eventually, Charlie. Wipe out everything. The world is run by idiots, Charlie."

Charlie let it rest there for more than a minute. Then he said, "Meanwhile, M.L.?"

Heimrich came back from wherever, gloomily, he had been.

"Yes," he said. "Meanwhile you and I are in the retail business, Charlie. Before he went out for his walk, Dr. Tennant looked at his watch, his wife says. It doesn't seem to have made any particular impression on her, at the moment. She just happened to remember it when I was talking to her."

Forniss said, "Mmmm."

"Perhaps," Heimrich said, "to check on an appointment he had? To meet somebody at the bottom of a flight of stairs, Charlie? Who, do you suppose?"

Forniss shook his head. Then he said, "Let's see. Miss Jameson had gone up to her room to lie down when the doctor went out for his walk. Anyway, she says she did and nobody says she didn't. Mrs. Tennant went up, she says, about the time her husband went out. Jameson went into Cold Harbor to buy cigarettes. Had trouble finding a place open. I had one of the boys check that. Only place open Sunday afternoons is one of the drugstores. Two of them in the town, and they alternate at being open on Sunday afternoons. The one open—called Browne's Pharmacy—sold quite a few cigarettes this afternoon. Mostly, the way the clerk remembers it, a pack or two at a time. One or two cartons, he thinks. One of them was maybe Kents King Size. Man insisted on the soft pack. Jameson smokes Kents. Clerk doesn't remember what time. Had to be before three, because they close at three. Sure a man bought the carton of Kents. Hasn't any idea what he looked like. Not a regular customer, he thinks. Says they get sort of busy just before they close up on Sundays."

"And Rankin, a while after the doctor went out, went up to his own room," Heimrich said. "To go over some papers, he says. Why bring papers along when you're going to a party, do you suppose?"

Forniss didn't know. He said that lawyers, from what he knew of them, tended to be funny guys.

If they were all telling the truth, Heimrich thought, none of the people in The Tor had made an appointment with Dr. James Tennant. There was no special reason to think that all of them were telling the truth. Probably Ronald Jameson had driven into Cold Harbor and bought cigarettes. On the other hand, a lot of people smoke Kents, whatever the Surgeon General has to say. Reminded, Merton Heimrich lighted a cigarette.

"No telephone calls we've heard about. Nobody calling from outside and getting Dr. Tennant on the line and saying, 'Meet me at the foot of the stairs down to the lake. Be sure to hold onto the handrail going down.'"

"Not that we've been able to pin down," Forniss said. "Earlier, yes. People calling up to say they'd just heard the terrible news. Phones all over the place. Mr. Jameson

118

had a line of his own. Not listed. Extensions in his room and his office. Four or five extensions on the listed line. There's also a private line—one of these do-it-yourself sort of things—from the kitchen to the Frankels' apartment over the garage. Damn!"

The "damn" was rueful. Heimrich said, "Yes, Charlie? Think of something?"

"Nothing important, I guess," Forniss said. "Frankel seems to have seen Dr. Tennant standing at the head of those damn stairs. Thinks it was maybe about two-thirty. Sometime around then. Happened to look out a window in their apartment and saw somebody, he's pretty sure the doctor, standing there. Looking down."

"Just the doctor, Charlie? Nobody with him? Getting set to push, maybe?"

"Just the doctor. Just happened to see him. Didn't think anything about it. He'd been looking at TV, Frankel had. Got up to go to the head and happened to look out the window. Retired Navy man, Frankel says he is. Chief bos'n, he says. More likely bos'n first, I'd guess. Not that it matters."

Heimrich agreed that Frankel's rating when he had been in the Navy didn't matter.

"He didn't see anybody at the foot of the stairs?"

"Says not."

"Could he have?"

Charles Forniss didn't know. He had seen Frankel in the kitchen when he was asking all the servants if they had seen anything that afternoon. Frankel was the only one who had seen anything.

"All right," Forniss said. "Maybe I slipped up. Maybe I should have gone over to the apartment and looked out the window."

Heimrich said it didn't matter and that, anyway, it was not too late.

Forniss had come out of The Tor when Heimrich had come back from the hospital. They had met in the big paved parking area in front of the gray stone house. They were still standing there. There were three police cruisers in the turnaround, and a trooper was in one of them, listening to the radio. The other two were empty. A gray Chrysler Imperial was also in the parking area. It, too, was empty.

"Far end of the house, the garage is," Forniss said. "Want me to go have a look, M.L.?" He gestured toward the end of the house.

"We'll both go," Heimrich said, and they walked along an extension of the driveway from the turnaround. The drive curved away from the house, and away from the stairs down to the lake.

The garage was large and built, like the house, of stone. It was large enough, Heimrich thought, for half a dozen cars. There was an outside staircase at one end of it, and they went up the staircase. At the top of it they pressed a button and a bell rang, rather loudly, inside.

A wide-faced, sturdy woman opened the door. She had gray hair coiled on top of her head, and her broad face was red. She had blue eyes which were not particularly large. Heimrich said, "Mrs. Frankel?" and she said, "Who did you expect?" Then she looked at Lieutenant Forniss and said, "Oh, it's you again. What do you want this time?"

A tall man with broad shoulders showed up behind Mrs. Frankel. He said, "It's their job, Gretchen," and looked at Heimrich and Forniss. He said, "Noon again, Lieutenant," and, to Heimrich, "You'd be the inspector, yes? Told the lieutenant everything I know about it, but come on in."

They went in. The room held a matching set of sofa and two chairs, all three done in a flowered pattern.

There was a heavy table in front of the sofa and, in a corner of the room, a smaller table. The smaller table's top was covered with little porcelain objects, most of them in the shapes of various animals. The gray carpet stretched from wall to wall. Everything in the room was almost excessively neat. "It was all very tidy." Something like that, anyway. Something Susan had quoted.

There was no television in the tidy room.

"This window you looked out when you saw Dr. Tennant, Mr. Frankel," Heimrich said. "In this room?"

"In the den," Mrs. Frankel said. "Where the TV is. He's always looking at ball games and things like that. All Sunday afternoons he looks at ball games. All kinds of ball games."

"All right, Gretchen," Frankel said. "I'll show you, yes?"

They followed him through the living room and into a corridor and into a smaller room which opened off the corridor.

There was a big television set in this room, which evidently was the "den." There was a black leather chair, which had been much sat on, in front of the set. There were newspapers on the floor beside the black chair. Mrs. Frankel, who had followed them out of the living room, brushed past them. She said, "Mess. All the time a mess," and picked the newspapers up and carried them out of the den.

There was one wide window in the room, and Heimrich went to it. He could look down at the beginning of the brick staircase; the top of the stairs was perhaps fifty yards away. He could not see the bottom of the staircase. He moved to one side and looked diagonally through the windowpane. He could see more of the stairs, but not to the bottom of them.

Heimrich turned back.

"It was from here you saw Dr. Tennant, Mr. Frankel?"

"Yes, Inspector. From where you are. Like I told the lieutenant, he was just standing there."

"Looking down the stairs?"

"Like I told the lieutenant. Yes."

"The window was closed?"

"Yes. There is a wind. It blows things around."

Heimrich said, "If you don't mind, Mr. Frankel," and opened the window. By leaning out of it, he could just see the bottom of the staircase. A trooper was sitting on a rock outcrop at the bottom of the stairs. He was, as Heimrich had supposed he would be, smoking a cigarette. He did not seem to be doing anything else. Presumably Asa Purvis had detailed him there. The young are diligent. Heimrich turned from the window.

"By the way, Mr. Frankel," Heimrich said, "you knew the condition of the railing, I understand. That it was rusting loose? And told Miss Jameson about it?"

"Been that way the last couple of years," Frankel said. "My business to know about things like that, yes? I told her, sure."

"Her? Not Mr. Jameson?"

"Didn't use to bother him much," Frankel said. "Didn't like to be bothered. Left things mostly to his sister, way it was. Mind closing the window, Inspector? Blows things around."

Heimrich turned back to the open window. He started to pull down the lower pane. He stopped when it was halfway closed.

A starter was grinding from the direction of the turn-around in front of the big house. The engine caught almost at once. It was a heavy engine and caught with a roar. Heimrich opened the window fully and leaned out of it. The corner of the house cut off his view of most of the turnaround. Then a big gray car backed into sight. It

122

turned and went down the drive, gravel spurting under its rear tires.

The trooper in the police car used his starter, and the engine caught. Another trooper ran out of the house toward the police car, which was already backing toward its own turn down the drive.

"Mr. Rankin seems to be leaving us," Heimrich said, and went out of the den, walking fast. Forniss went after him.

When they had gone down the stairs, Heimrich went into a trot and Forniss ran after him. When they reached the turnaround, the police cruiser had left it, with gravel spurting. And the starter of a second police car was grinding.

"Hold it," Heimrich shouted to the trooper behind the wheel of the second cruiser. The sound of the starter stopped.

"The car which went after the Chrysler," Heimrich said. "What's its number?"

"Four-twenty, Inspector. Four-two-oh. You don't want we should—?"

"No," Heimrich said. He went on to the Buick. He switched the radio on and got the usual clatter of voices. He took the transmitter off the hook.

"Car Ten calling dispatch," Heimrich said. "Come in, K. Car One-oh calling—"

"Troop K dispatch," a voice said through the clatter. "Come in, Ten. One-oh, come in."

"Heimrich. Car Four-twenty—repeat, Car Four-two-oh—is following a gray Chrysler Imperial on Route Eleven F. South on Eleven F, probably. Get Four-two-oh and direct it not—repeat not—to stop the Chrysler. Do not use siren. Follow at a distance and report movements of Chrysler. If it crosses city line, or appears to be about to, turn over to city police. Message clear?"

"Message received, Inspector. Follow but do not impede."

"Yes," Heimrich said and put the transmitter back on its hook. He remembered he had forgotten to say, "Over and out," which dispatchers expect as their due. He got out of the Buick.

"On the run, looks like," Forniss said.

"Not too far with a tail on him," Heimrich said. "Interesting to see where he runs to, naturally. My hunch is—"

He did not finish. A half truck was crunching up the drive. There were two men in it, both in work clothes. As the truck turned to park, Heimrich could see the lettering on the side of its cab. It read, "Denny & Co., General Contractors."

"Men I called," Forniss said. "Men with the dragline." He walked toward the truck.

The man who got out of the truck appeared to be in his sixties. He was lean and weathered. He said, "You the man called us? Furnish? Something like that?"

"Forniss."

"So all right. Get the gear out, Ted. Where's this damn lake?"

"Over there," Forniss said, and pointed. "You'll have to go down a long flight of steps. The railing's loose, so watch it."

"Bring it along, Ted," the weathered man said to the larger, and much younger, man who was unloading a dragline from the truck. He went off in the direction Forniss had pointed out. Ted wrapped a considerable length of rope over a shoulder and took out a metal piece which looked somewhat like a big rake. He carried the line and the drag as if they were heavy, and went after the lean, weathered man.

124

"All they'll do'll be worry the fish, probably," Forniss said.

"Probably," Heimrich said, and walked off toward the house. Forniss went with him.

Asa Purvis opened the door for them.

"It's my fault, sir," Purvis said. "Should've stopped him. Only, I saw you and the lieutenant drive up and I thought we were covered and—well, I had to go, sir. I mean, you know how it is sometimes."

"We all have to go sometimes, Asa," Heimrich said. "Don't worry about it."

"He'd just been wandering around," Asa Purvis said. "Restless like. Looking out of windows and that sort of thing. But I didn't get the idea he was going to—well, going to light out."

"None of us did," Heimrich said, and went on into the house. He went into the long drawing room. There were only a few coals left in the fireplace. Ursula Jameson was sitting in front of it. She had changed from slacks to a black dress. She had smoothed her gray hair. Her nose jutted over lightly rouged lips. When Heimrich and Forniss were still half the room from her, Ursula Jameson said, "I've been waiting for you, Inspector. Where have you been?"

Heimrich did not answer until he had pulled a chair up at the end of the sofa and sat down in it. Forniss went to lean against the fireplace.

"At the hospital, Miss Jameson," Heimrich said. "Dr. Tennant is still unconscious, and they don't seem to expect any immediate change. Your niece is quieter now. Still in shock, of course, but quieter."

"Those awful stairs," Ursula said. "I kept telling Arthur. Telling him over and over. He—when it was things about the house, he just let things drift by. Because things get to be too much trouble. You're a young man. You wouldn't know."

Merton Heimrich does not think of himself as a particularly young man. He let it go—let it, he thought, drift past him. He said, "I suppose not, Miss Jameson. You've been waiting for me, you say?"

"That Rankin man," she said. "Did he run away? Did you let him run away?"

"He left," Heimrich said. "He wasn't under detention. Legally, quite free to go where he likes. As all of you are, of course."

"Well," Ursula Jameson said, "maybe you know your business, Inspector." The doubt in her voice was noticeable.

"I hope so," Heimrich said. "You've been waiting for me, you say. Have you thought of something you want to tell us? About your brother's death? About Dr. Tennant's fall?"

"My brother was killed," she said. "Murdered. I don't know anything about Jim Tennant's accident. Except that the railing came loose. My brother should have had it repaired a long time ago. I kept telling him about it. Of course, the doctor should have looked where he was going."

"Was he inclined not to?" Heimrich asked her, and she said, "What?"

"To look where he was going," Heimrich said.

"He walked around thinking," she said. "I will say that. Almost, sometimes, as if he were reading something when he walked. If that's what you mean."

"What I'm asking about. Just trying to find things out. You mean, abstracted? Not watching where he was putting his feet?"

"You could call it that if you wanted to. He was that

126

way today after—after the awful thing about Arthur. Didn't you sense that?"

"No," Heimrich said. "Of course, I met him for the first time today."

"Last night," she said. "You must have met him last night. Or did Arthur forget to introduce you? He did forget sometimes."

Heimrich said he didn't remember meeting Dr. James Tennant. He added that there were a lot of people at the party last night.

"Arthur's idea," she said. "If he'd left it to me, the way he did most things. Not that arranging the party wasn't left to me. Getting everything in and all those extra people. And the candles. Have you any idea how many candles we had to have?"

Heimrich shook his head. He thought, She's showing her age. People get rattled sometimes as they get old.

"Ten dozen," she said. "Ten dozen candles. And do you think it's easy to find a suckling pig? And get it roasted properly?"

"I'm sure it wasn't," Heimrich said. He found his mind tending to wander. He wondered if the men pulling a line behind a rowboat were doing anything more helpful than disturbing fish. He wondered whether he had been right in his guess about Goeffrey Rankin. He brought his mind back—back, apparently, to the difficulty of getting a suckling pig properly roasted. With, of course, an apple in its mouth. His mind stayed there only for an instant.

"You said you'd been waiting for me, Miss Jameson. Had you thought of something you wanted to tell me? Something you'd remembered? About your brother's death?"

"Murder," she said. "Why don't you call it murder?

You think I'm a silly old woman, don't you?"

"No," Heimrich said. "Something you remembered? Perhaps something that, when you'd thought it over, seemed to have more significance than it had when it first happened?"

"It didn't really happen," she said. "It was just a dream. I'm sure it was just a dream. I was just sitting here, brooding about it. But I'm sure it was just a dream."

"Suppose," Heimrich said, "you tell me about this dream, Miss Jameson."

9

She looked at the almost-dead fire, as if she expected to find her dream in it. Then, instead of telling about her dream, she got up and walked to the padded cord on the wall and pulled it sharply. There is no uncertainty about where she is putting her feet, Heimrich thought, as he had thought the night before when he watched her walk up the crowded room.

She walked back to the sofa and sat on it, and looked down the room toward the end where the bar had been. Barnes came in from that end of the room. When he had come part way up the room he said, "Yes, Miss Jameson?"

"The fire's burned down," Ursula Jameson said. "Will you build it up again, Barnes? It's getting cold in here."

It did not seem cold in there to Merton Heimrich. Barnes said, "Yes," and went down the room again. Ursula Jameson opened an oblong box on the table in front of her and took a cigarette out of it. She put the cigarette between her lightly rouged lips. Heimrich got up from his chair and flicked his lighter and held the flame out to the cigarette. He thought that the black-clad woman was postponing telling him about her dream.

Barnes came back with a filled canvas log carrier. He knelt on the hearth and put kindling on the faint embers. He put logs on top of the kindling. He took a brassbound bellows from a rack on the hearth. He blew on the embers with the bellows and, after a little time, the kindling caught. He stood up. He said, "Will there be anything else, Miss Jameson?"

"A Scotch and water," Ursula said. "And just one lump of ice."

Barnes said, "Yes'm, Miss Jameson," and started toward the far door, the now-empty log carrier dangling from his hand. Ursula Jameson said, "Wait," after he had gone half a dozen steps. He stopped and turned back. Ursula said, "You, Inspector?" without looking at him, looking at the jumping flames which were edging around the logs.

"No," Heimrich said, and added "thanks" to it.

She looked up at Charles Forniss, standing with his shoulders against the fireplace wall. She did not say anything. Forniss said, "I guess not, Miss Jameson."

She said, "All right, Barnes. Only one cube of ice," and Barnes said, "Yes, Miss Jameson. One cube," and went on down the room.

She drew on her cigarette and continued to look at the fire. For such a big fireplace, the fire drew well, Heimrich thought. He said, "This dream, Miss Jameson?"

"Probably it's nothing," she said. "Just a dream. When I was—"

Barnes came toward them again from the far end of the room. He carried a tray with a glass on it. There was pale liquid in the glass and one cube of ice. He put the tray down on the table in front of Ursula Jameson, and she said, "Thank you, Barnes." He said, "Thank you, Miss Jameson," and went back the way he had come.

It was, Heimrich thought, a little as if they were acting in a play, and the play late in its run so that movements and lines had become stereotyped. He watched Ursula Jameson lift her glass and sip from it. Again he said, "This dream, Miss Jameson?"

"Probably," she said, "it was just as I was waking up. I read somewhere that people dream mostly when they are just waking up. Probably what I heard was—oh, it could have been the maid knocking on my door to tell me she had heard Jeff Rankin calling the police. And I got it all mixed up. Dreams are such mixed-up things, aren't they?"

She looked at Heimrich, who said, "Yes, Miss Jameson. They're often mixed-up things."

"In the dream," she said, "it seemed to be earlier. Seemed just to be getting light. I thought it waked me up, but I suppose I just dreamed waking up. It's all vague—terribly vague. I dreamed I thought, But it's Sunday. She's not supposed to come on Sunday."

She looked into the fire, which now was burning well. She sipped again from her glass. Her cigarette was smoldering in the tray and she stubbed it out. It was, Merton Heimrich thought, as if she were redreaming this dream of hers. He did not say anything.

"She ought to have something done about that car," Ursula told the fire she was looking into. "It makes such a dreadful racket. But it wasn't really the car, of course. It was the maid knocking on my door to wake me up and tell me—tell me she thought something had happened because—"

She stopped speaking and shook her head. Then she looked at Heimrich. "I'm not usually like this, Inspector," she said. "It's been a bad day. A terrible day."

131

"Yes, Miss Jameson," Heimrich said. "It's been a bad day. You thought—dreamed, I mean—that a car had wakened you just when it was beginning to get light this morning? A noisy car? Whose car, Miss Jameson?"

"Whenever she came here to work with Arthur," she said, "you could hear the car when it first turned into the drive. Rattling and banging. Almost anywhere in the house you were you could hear that car of hers. It got so that at a few minutes before nine I got to listening for that car to come banging in."

"Miss Selby usually came around nine?" Heimrich said.

"Four days a week," Ursula Jameson said. "She doesn't come on Wednesdays. Did I say it was Dorothy Selby's car?"

"No," Heimrich said. "I've heard the car she drives is rather noisy. It was her car in this dream of yours, wasn't it?"

"It was just the maid knocking on the door," she said. "It—it just seemed like a car in the dream."

"Just as it was getting light," Heimrich said. "That's the way it was in this dream of yours? You didn't dream you looked at your watch? Or at a clock by your bed?"

"There wasn't anything about a clock in my dream," she told him. "There isn't any time in dreams. Oh, sometimes they seem to go on for hours, but Jim Tennant says they often last only seconds. They've run tests of some kind, he says. He says the tests show when people are dreaming. He says they think everybody dreams but don't always remember the dreams. And that sometimes when they do remember it's hours after they're awake."

"You just remembered this dream?"

"It sort of came back after lunch. When I was lying down. Perhaps I dozed off and—and dreamed the same dream again. Could it have been that way, do you think?"

"I don't know," Heimrich said.

"Perhaps it was while I was dozing that the doctor fell down those awful stairs," she said, and seemed to shiver in front of the now exuberant fire. "Will he remember what happened, Inspector? Remember any of this awful day?"

"They don't know yet," Heimrich told her. "A specialist is coming up from—"

The telephone at the upper end of the room rang. It rang only once. Forniss had started toward it but stopped. Then Barnes came in at the far end of the room. This time he did not walk up the room, but called from just inside it. "There's a telephone call for you, Inspector," Barnes said, raising his voice. "You can take it there, sir."

Heimrich walked up the room toward the telephone in the cabinet. Ursula Jameson sat and looked into the fire. Heimrich spoke his name into the telephone.

"Trooper Snyder, T. J., sir. Car Four-two-oh. We've been following a gray Chrysler Imperial"—he gave the license number—"with radio instructions not to interfere with its movements."

"Yes, Snyder."

"Subject car proceeded to Cold Harbor. In the town it proceeded up Vine Street for about a mile."

He paused.

"Proceed, Trooper," Heimrich said, and Snyder said, "Huh?"

"Go ahead," Heimrich told him. "The car went up Vine Street. You went after it, keeping your distance. Do you think the driver saw you?"

"Could be, I guess. We were cruising along slow like, as instructed. We were maybe a quarter mile behind him most of the time. Subject car wasn't going fast, sir. Just sort of loafing along."

"Yes?"

"We proceeded after subject car in Vine Street for seven tenths of a mile, sir. Subject car—"

"All right, Snyder. You're not in court. You mean the Chrysler. You followed it up Vine Street for seven tenths of a mile. Then?"

"He turned into a driveway, sir. Off to the right. There was a sign at the foot of the driveway. It said, 'Florence Selby, Realtor,' Inspector."

"Go ahead, Snyder."

"We pulled up to the curb just before we got to this driveway," Snyder said. "Rightly, there isn't any curb. It's more a road than a street, sir. We stopped maybe fifty feet before we got to the driveway. I got out and walked to the bottom of the driveway, leaving Trooper Gilson, B. T., in the car. I looked up the driveway, sir. There's a big lilac bush there and I sort of stayed behind it, well as I could. I could see pretty good. Way I got it, sir, driver of the subject car wasn't supposed to know we'd been trailing him."

"He probably did," Heimrich said. "He drove up to the house and stopped the car in the turnaround. And, Snyder?"

"Tall man," Snyder said. "He got out of the car and a girl—a young woman, sir—ran out of the house and—well, they hugged each other, Inspector. Then they walked up to the house and went into it. He had an arm around her all the time, sir. Once they were in the house I couldn't see any more, Inspector, so I waited maybe five minutes, and went back to the car. So we drove on past the driveway maybe a hundred yards, so's we wouldn't be in plain sight if he came out. The street dead-ends a couple of blocks up, so we figured when subject car left it would go back the way we'd come, so we turned the car around and parked headed what we figured would be the right way and waited a while. Maybe about ten minutes. We could see the foot of this driveway from where we'd parked. Maybe about ten minutes it was, and the subject car came out of the driveway and turned back toward the center of town. We gave it a good start and followed. On the main street, there's a restaurant. Just called 'The Tavern,' sir. He drove into the parking lot and got out of the car and went into the restaurant. We drove past, slow like, and Benny got a chance to look in. He was on that side of the car, sir. He could see the bar through the window and there were three or four men standing at it and he's pretty sure one of them was the driver of the subject car. So—*hey!*"

"Yes?"

"I'm in a booth across the street. He's just come out of the place—couldn't have had more than one drink—and he's walking around to the car. Maybe I'd better—"

"Yes, Trooper," Heimrich said, "I think you'd better."

The receiver clicked in his ear. He hung up and walked back to the center of the room—to the leaping fire and Miss Ursula Jameson sitting erect on the sofa in front of it. She had nearly finished her drink. She had lighted another cigarette. Heimrich looked at the watch on his wrist. It was a little after seven o'clock. He looked toward the french doors. It was growing dark outside. Soon it would be too dark for Denny & Co. to go on dragging the lake, unless they'd brought a powerful light with them.

"We'll be going now, Miss Jameson," Heimrich said. "The lieutenant and I. There'll be a couple of troopers around to see that nothing else happens."

"If they can," Ursula Jameson said. She looked away from the fire and up at Heimrich. "You're not getting anywhere with it, are you?"

"If they can," Heimrich agreed. "We'll probably be back tomorrow, Miss Jameson."

She looked back at the fire and moved her head

slowly from side to side. She did not say anything; Heimrich doubted whether she had heard what he had said last. When he and Forniss had gone a little way up the long room, Ursula Jameson said, "Ring for Barnes, will you?"

Forniss pulled on the padded cord.

They went out into the gathering darkness. The wind which whipped at them was a cold wind. They got into the Buick. Heimrich put the ignition key in but did not turn it.

"We'll wait a bit," Heimrich said.

They waited for a little more than ten minutes. Then headlights came up the drive toward them, throwing a glare against trees on one side and then the other as the drive twisted.

When the big gray Chrysler turned to park, the lights did not fall on the unlighted Buick.

Geoffrey Rankin got out of his car and walked toward the house and into it. Heimrich waited another minute or two before he turned the ignition key and the Buick's engine came alive. He switched on the lights. He did not, immediately, put the car in gear.

"Rankin apparently just drove in to see Miss Selby," Heimrich said. "Stopped for a drink afterward."

Forniss said, "Yeah?"

"Went to the Vine Street house in Cold Harbor," Heimrich said. "You think Miss Jameson just dreamed up something, Charlie?"

"That Volks of Miss Selby's is supposed to make quite a racket," Forniss said. "Needs a tune-up, sounds like."

Heimrich said it did sound like that, from what they'd heard. What they'd heard did not, of course, include the Volks itself.

The Buick's engine purred. A flashlight came toward them, bobbing with a man's walking movement. The thin weathered man and his bigger companion came into the Buick's headlight beams. The big man wasn't carrying anything.

Forniss got out of the car and walked toward them. The thin older man said, "Getting too dark. Back tomorrow," and the two walked on to their truck.

"Didn't find anything?" Forniss said, knowing the answer.

The thin man said, "Nope," and got into the truck. The truck's starter ground. The motor caught, hesitated; caught again with a roar. Forniss walked back to the Buick. He did not get into it.

"Drop you?" Heimrich said.

Forniss shook his head.

"Get one of the cruisers to take me up to the barracks," Forniss said. "May as well get the report moving."

There are always reports to get moving.

"All right," Heimrich said. He ran up the window on the side Forniss stood on. Then he ran it down again.

"Tell you what, Charlie," Heimrich said. "While you're at the barracks, you might check back in the records. See what we've got on this accident Janet Jameson had a couple of years ago. Horse threw her into a stone fence, way we get it."

Forniss looked in at him. Forniss's eyebrows went up.

"Jameson's second wife," Heimrich said. "She died of head injuries. Apparently got thrown headfirst into this stone fence."

It was several seconds before Forniss spoke. Then all he said was. "O.K., M.L. I'll check it out."

10

Susan had flames jumping in the fireplace of the long, low house above the Hudson. She had been sitting in front of the fire reading, and delighting in, S. N. Behrman's *People in a Diary*. When she heard the crunch of the Buick's tires on gravel, she put the book down and went to the door and was there, looking up, when Merton Heimrich opened it. For a second or two she studied his face before he leaned down to kiss her.

"It's been a long day," she said. "You need a drink."

"It has," Merton said. "I do." He walked over to the fireplace and stood in front of it and rubbed his hands together. He had had the heater on in the car and his hands were not really cold. The movement of his hands was a symbol; a symbol that summer was over; an acknowledgment that tonight they would not have drinks on the terrace. Tomorrow, if he had time tomorrow, he might as well stow the terrace furniture.

"I'll—" Merton said but Susan shook her head at him.

"No, I will," she said. "You've had a long Sunday. It would be a good evening for hot buttered rum. Only we haven't any rum, and I've no idea how one butters it."

Merton sat down in one of the two deep chairs which faced the fire. "There's something about a hot poker in it, I think," he said.

"Sounds rather gritty," Susan said and went into the kitchen to make their martinis. She brought them back and put the tray on the table. She sat beside the big man, who had stretched his legs out, feet toward the fire. They clicked glasses.

They sat for a moment in silence, sipping cold gin and a very little vermouth from chilled glasses with the faint tang of twisted lemon peel rubbed on their edges.

"I can't get over that bow-and-arrow bit," Susan said. "It seems so—so archaic. But last night everything did, didn't it? She's very ugly, isn't she?"

When people have been long enough together, transitions become unnecessary.

"Well," Merton said, "she's got rather a long nose. Also, she's been out in the sun a lot. Did you and the Jacksons and Alden finish the last nine?"

"Too blowy, we decided," Susan told him. "So we had lunch and I came home and did some things around the house. And took a nap, it being Sunday. And, of course, waited." She sipped from her glass. "I do one hell of a lot of waiting," she told the glass and the fire. "A while back I hoped—"

She did not finish, or need to. Merton Heimrich knew what she had hoped—that when he became an inspector he would work during set hours, staying at a desk. It had not turned out that way. Heimrich had never thought it would; nor, knowing him, had Susan.

"A man fell down a flight of stairs," Merton said. "Brick stairs down to a lake. He trusted to a handrail and it came loose in his hand."

He took a pack of cigarettes from his pocket and loosened two cigarettes and held the pack out to Susan. She took a cigarette and he took the other, and he lighted both. "We smoke too much," Susan said, and drew deeply. She said, "An accident? And was he hurt?"

"It looked like being an accident," Merton told her. "Yes, he was hurt badly. Fractured skull; probable brain damage. He's still unconscious. Was when I checked last anyway."

"So if he had something to remember he won't remember it? Planned that way?"

"I don't know, dear," Merton Heimrich told his wife. "We're just digging around, Charlie and I."

He finished his drink. Susan moved in her deep chair. "No," Merton said, "my turn."

"I thought they were all right," Susan said. "Almost no vermouth."

"They were fine," Merton said, and got up out of the deep chair. "You've been playing golf. Building a fire. I've been sitting, mostly. Asking questions."

"There are glasses in the freezing compartment," Susan said. "You think another log?"

Heimrich looked into the fire. He thought another log wouldn't do it any harm. He carried the tray into the kitchen and mixed martinis and poured from the mixer into chilled glasses and twisted lemon peel over drinks and rubbed it, gently, around the rims of the glasses. He carried the tray back to the long living room of the house which once had been a barn and put it on the table between them. He put another log in the right place on the fire. He sat and, again, they clicked their glasses together.

140

"The man who fell downstairs," Heimrich said, "was a physician. A psychiatrist. He's a few years older than his wife."

"You're a few years older than I am," Susan said. "It comes out right that way. Not that difference in age has to make a lot of difference, one way or the other. Except—"

She paused and drank. She put her glass down on the table.

"Of course," she said, "fifty years is a lot of difference. It must have been almost that."

"Apparently Jameson liked it that way," Heimrich said. "His second wife was a good deal younger than he was. Not as much, of course, as Dorothy Selby would have been."

Susan raised her eyebrows and shook her head slightly.

"The girl he was going to marry," Merton told her.

"Of course," Susan said. "That child. That poor child." She sipped again. "I guess," she said.

"Not in the other sense," Merton said. "She inherits what may be a great deal of money. From Jameson."

She said, "Oh." She said, "Not his sister?"

"The house and the land," Merton said. "Apparently she's what they call independently wealthy."

"It would be nice to be independently wealthy," Susan told the glass in her hand. "Then I wouldn't have to wait so much. We could go some place on a ship. One with no murders, I mean." She looked at him. "You're waiting for something, aren't you?" Susan Heimrich said. "Dinner? It's a casserole, and it's in the oven." She sipped again. "On 'Warm,' " she said.

"Charlie may call," Merton said.

"And you'll go out again?"

Heimrich said he shouldn't think so. He said he thought they were through for the day.

They finished their drinks. They decided against third rounds, Merton after a moment's hesitation. "We can have it here," Susan said. "It's comfortable here. Fires are the one good thing about autumn."

They had the casserole, which turned out to be a ragout, in front of the fire. They had finished it and little rum cakes and were drinking coffee when the telephone rang. Susan moved in her chair, but Merton was out of his. Susan smiled at the fire and shook her head slightly at it and thought, It's Charlie Forniss, or he thinks it is. Telephones ringing in their house are usually Susan's to answer.

Merton said, "Heimrich," into the telephone and then, "Yes, Charlie?" He listened for a second and said, "No, I didn't suppose there would be much. Just an accident. One of those things that happen to people who ride horses."

Heimrich had not been on a horse in several years, although when he was a very young State trooper in western New York horses still were ridden.

"Thing is," Forniss said, "seems the horse didn't fall. Just balked a jump in this meadow of theirs. Mrs. Jameson—Janet Jameson, that is—went over its head into a stone wall. Way she tells it, the horse was all right when she rode up. Just munching grass. Mrs. Jameson, though, was dead."

"She, Charlie? Who was she? And when did this happen?"

"Miss Jameson. Miss Ursula Jameson. Two years ago last spring. The first decent day in a long time, so they decided to go riding. In that meadow the other side of the lake. Part of the Jameson land, the meadow is. The stable was over there, then. Not there any more, M.L. Jameson seems to have had it torn down after his wife was killed. He sold off the horses, including the stallion

142

who refused the jump. He hadn't ridden much himself for a good many years, the way I get it."

"He wasn't riding with his wife that day?"

"Seems he was in New York. Banquet of some Anglo-American outfit. He went in that morning. They had to page him at the dinner to tell him about his wife. The way the trooper got it. The man who checked the accident out. Didn't check very hard, apparently. Just got the outline. I can't say I blame him, M.L."

"All right, Charlie. Tell me what he did get."

What the trooper had got, almost entirely from Miss Ursula Jameson, was this:

The accident which had taken Janet Jameson's life had occurred early in the long Memorial Day weekend. Memorial Day had fallen on a Saturday that year: the following Monday, June first, had been the official day for commemoration. Jameson had gone into New York for the dinner a little before midday on Friday. Ursula Jameson and her sister-in-law had been alone in the big house Friday afternoon, except for the servants.

"Not the ones they've got there now," Forniss interjected. "Different set altogether, according to the trooper's list. Except the Frankels. He's not what you would call a servant. Caretaker's more like it."

"Even Barnes?"

"Yep. Man named Brooks they had then. Seem to run to B's, don't they? Of course, The Tor's a pretty isolated place. Hard to keep a staff in a place like that, I guess. Anyway—"

"So what the trooper got came from Miss Jameson?" Heimrich said, and got "Yep" for an answer. The "Yep" was modified by "Pretty much, the way it looks." Heimrich said, "Go ahead, Charlie."

In late afternoon of that Friday, Janet Jameson had said that, since it was the first nice day they'd had in a month, she thought she'd go riding and asked Ursula if she wanted to come along.

"We'd felt cooped up," Ursula Jameson had told the trooper who was conducting routine enquiries. She had told Frankel, who was working in the garden, to row across and saddle the horses—Alphonse for Janet, and her mare.

"Alphonse?" Heimrich said.

Forniss agreed it was a funny name for a stallion, but there it was. And the mare's name was Ophelia.

Frankel had rowed across the lake and saddled the two horses and tethered them. He had rowed back and returned to his gardening. Ursula and Janet had driven over to the stable.

Heimrich said, "Driven, Charlie? Across the lake?"

There was another way to the stable, in which the Jamesons then had four horses, and the ten-acre meadow which surrounded them. A town road led off NY 11F about a mile south of The Tor. It passed the Jameson property on the far side. A private road led off it, to the stable and the big meadow; towards the lake. Since the private road was unpaved and it was still spring, they had gone in the Jeep. They had not planned to stay long because "the others were coming up."

"The others, Charlie?"

"The Tennants. The old man's son. They were due for dinner, the way the trooper got it. Up for the weekend. Anyway—"

The two women had driven around to the stable and found their horses saddled and tethered. According to Ursula Jameson, they had mounted at about four-thirty.

"The trooper got that verbatim," Forniss said. "One of the few things he did. Want I should read it?"

"Yes, Charlie."

"So she said, 'It had been a wet April and the grass was already pretty high. There's a bridle path which more

144

or less circles the meadow, and Frankel keeps it fairly clean. Frankel exercises the horses, but he hadn't got around to it for about a week, and they were frisky. Particularly Alphonse, of course. My brother never liked Janet's riding him, but she had her own way. Mostly she did, actually. The mare was a little jumpy too, and I kept to the path. Janet—well, Janet liked to jump. So did her horse, come to that.

" 'She rode off up the rise and then down on the other side, and I knew she was headed toward the stone fence. Yes, it runs between the main pasture and the second pasture beyond. It's always been there, as far as I know. In our grandfather's time they were still farming, I suppose, and the fence was to divide the fields. It's an easy jump. A few years ago I used to take it often. Too old for it now.

" 'Anyway, she went up the rise and down on the other side. The mare wanted to follow Alphonse, but I wouldn't let her. I just jogged along on the path. Later I heard a loud whinny from beyond the rise—a scream, almost. The way they sound when they're frightened. It worried me, so I rode over. Yes, up the rise, until I could look down toward the wall. And—do I have to tell about it, Trooper?' "

Apparently the trooper had asked her to tell about it.

" 'The horse was standing on the near side of the wall. Janet wasn't on him. Then I saw where he had torn up the turf with his hooves. This side of the fence. And then—then I saw Janet. She was lying with her head against the stone fence and she wasn't moving. I rode down and—and her head was crushed against the wall. I got down and ran to her but—but even before I got to her I knew it was no use. Knew she was dead. So—I don't remember at all well. You can see I wouldn't. I think I thought of rowing back across the lake, but then I remembered the boat would be on the other side.

So I must have ridden back to the stable and driven around in the Jeep. I—I can't tell you any more, Trooper. Don't you see that?'

"That's the verbatim," Forniss said. "According to what Frankel told the trooper, she came up the drive damn fast in the Jeep and stopped it and jumped out, and then, Frankel says, she began to scream. Jameson's son had just got to the house, and she told them what had happened. Frankel and the son started telephoning for help. Called the local police in Cold Harbor, and they got onto us. Called the hospital for an ambulance. Called the sheriff's office too, come to that. When they all got there, it was the way Miss Jameson had said. Her horse was still saddled and loose. So was the stallion. Stallion wasn't hurt. Both the horses were eating grass, one near the stable, the other near the stone fence. Mrs. Jameson was dead. Head all bashed in. They got hold of Jameson, but it took them quite a while. His son did that. The Tennants showed up a little later, according to what the troopers got. Jameson had gone in by train. He hired a car to come back. Didn't get there until around ten. About the size of it, M.L."

Heimrich said, "Mmmm." For some seconds he said nothing more. Then he said, "Frankel rowed across and saddled the horses. Then he rowed back and tied up the boat. Did he see the two women take off in the Jeep?"

"Nothing about that in the report, M.L. Like I said, obvious accident. They—well, they just went through the routine. You think that wasn't enough?"

"Now, Charlie," Heimrich said. "I don't know, naturally. Probably seemed like enough at the time, anyway. We'll maybe try to check more tomorrow. You may as well knock it off. Get yourself some sleep."

Forniss said, "O.K., M.L.," and hung up. Heimrich stood, looking down at the telephone.

"Do you have to go out again tonight?" Susan asked him from across the room.

For some seconds, Merton continued merely to look at the telephone. Then he said, "No. Not tonight," but he still stood by the telephone. Then he dialed a number with which the day had made him familiar. After three rings he got, "The Tor." He knew the voice. He said, "Heimrich, Barnes. I'd like to speak to Mr. Rankin."

"They're having dinner, sir. Miss Jameson and Mr. Jameson and Mr. Rankin."

"Tell Mr. Rankin I won't keep him long," Heimrich said and got an agreeing "Sir." He waited. After several minutes, he got, "Evening, Inspector. You wanted to talk to me?"

"Just to ask you how you found Miss Selby this afternoon. When you drove over to see her."

"And you had me followed," Rankin said. "Rather obviously. You might tell that trooper of yours that the lilac bush isn't all that good a cover."

"All right," Heimrich said. "I'll tell him. How did you find Miss Selby on your—call it sympathy call?"

"Doing as well as can be expected."

Heimrich sighed. He made his sigh highly audible.

"All right," Rankin said. "She's shaken up, of course. She'll survive it."

"I wouldn't be surprised," Heimrich said. "You consoled her?"

"Tried to, I suppose. You're reading things in, aren't you, Inspector? Things I told you weren't there? She's a cousin of mine, after all. Family, you could call it."

"A distant cousin, you said," Heimrich told him. "Let's see. It was you yourself who said—what was it?— not within the bounds of consanguinity. Something like that, wasn't it?"

"I don't remember, Inspector. Perhaps something like that. Mrs. Selby and my mother were second cousins,

I think. Something like that. Which makes Dot and me —well, you figure it out, Inspector. No closer than—oh, than Eleanor and Franklin Roosevelt, at a guess."

Heimrich said he saw. He said, "But you did drive over to see her. Felt a duty to a distant relative, Mr. Rankin?"

"We are friends," Rankin said. "I told you that, too. A few years ago we saw a bit of each other. When she was—oh, about twenty. I took her around a little. She was a damn pretty kid."

"She still is," Heimrich said. "A very attractive young woman."

"So?"

"So nothing in particular," Heimrich said. "You haven't seen so much of her recently, I gather. For about how long, would you say? That you haven't seen so much of each other, I mean?"

"A few years," Rankin said. "Three maybe. Maybe four."

"Since she started working for Mr. Jameson? As his secretary?"

"Nothing to do with it," Rankin said. His voice had sharpened. "Nothing to do with anything."

"All right," Heimrich said. "I didn't say it had, Mr. Rankin. Happen to know how long she's been acting as Mr. Jameson's secretary?"

"About three—" He stopped speaking. "Why don't you ask her that, Inspector?"

"Because, as you say, she's shaken up. Naturally. We try not to bother people who are—are grieving for somebody. If we can avoid it, of course. Went to work with Mr. Jameson before his second wife had her riding accident, would you say? Her fatal accident?"

"Listen," Rankin said, "I don't know anything about the Jamesons. Oh, that Jameson's previous wife was

148

killed in an accident. Dot told me about that, I think. Just—oh, just in passing. All that I know about the Jamesons is that you're forcing me to be a guest of theirs. Making me impose on Miss Jameson."

"Not forcing," Heimrich said. "Just asking, Mr. Rankin. Asking you to stay around until things get cleared up a little."

"And how long's that going to be?"

"Not too long, I hope. Perhaps not long at all. Good night, Mr. Rankin."

He hung up and went back to his chair by the fire.

"There's an old movie on at nine-thirty," Susan said. "One we've only seen twice. Well, maybe three times actually. It might be relaxing. Nobody gets killed in it, far's I can remember."

"I think small brandies would be even more relaxing," Heimrich said. "There's a poem you've said to me. I thought of it today. I've forgotten why. Something about something's being tidy?"

" 'It was all very tidy,' " Susan said. "Death's house, Merton. Robert Graves."

Merton Heimrich nodded his head and said that, of course, he remembered now. He went off to get them small brandies.

*　*　*　*

The wind had died down Monday morning and the sun was shining. There had not been a frost overnight. The flowers in Susan's garden were still alive, although, Merton Heimrich thought as he backed the Buick out of the garage, they looked a little daunted. He got to the headquarters of Troop K in Washington Hollow at about nine-thirty. Charles Forniss was already there; he had got the necessary routine started.

149

Geoffrey Rankin was listed in the Manhattan telephone directory as "lwyr." His office address was in the East Fifties. His "Res" was farther east, in the Sixties. A "good" address, by which was meant the address of somebody reasonably prosperous. Only his name was listed at the office address, so presumably he was not a member of a law firm. The New York City police were checking.

Forniss, who knows somebody almost everywhere, knew a man connected with the advertising business in New York. He had waked up the man he knew in his apartment—waked up the man and his wife—and the man had said, "What the hell at this hour, Charlie." It had not, however, been all that early.

He didn't know Ronald Jameson. Not personally. Oh, maybe he'd run into him once or twice. At the Advertising Club, it could be. Sure, he knew the firm of Jameson and Perkins by reputation. Not one of the biggest, but one that was getting along all right. "Hell, Charlie, they've got the Froth Soap account. Had it for a couple of years, anyway. And Froth Soap isn't hay, Charles my friend."

James Tennant, M.D., was a psychiatrist and neurologist. He belonged to several of the appropriate psychiatric and neurological societies. He had graduated in Medicine at Duke University's medical school and interned at the Duke University Hospital. He had interned in neurology at Johns Hopkins and in psychiatry at Harvard. "Highly qualified man."

The assurance of his qualification had come from Isadore Werkes, M.D., also a psychiatrist and neurologist, sometime consultant to the Office of the District Attorney, County of New York, and himself also highly qualified. Dr. Werkes knew Dr. Tennant only slightly; he knew of him very well, as did all physicians in their joint field. Dr. Werkes had declined to speculate on Dr. Tennant's probable income but assumed that it was adequate. Dr. Tennant was accredited to New York Hospital, Doctors Hospital and St. Vincent's.

Dr. Frank Wenning, who at present was presumably trying to determine the extent of Dr. Tennant's head injuries, was a neural surgeon. "One of the top men in the field," Dr. Werkes had said. He belonged to several surgical societies, including the one Dr. Werkes thought the most important among the Eastern societies.

Forniss did not know anybody in Cold Harbor, but the chief of Cold Harbor's small police force knew Mrs. Florence Selby. And Mrs. Selby was quite a girl. She had taken over her husband's real-estate business when he died. "Probably been running it all along, come to that."

She made "damn near half" of the real-estate sales in that part of Putnam County. She was on the school board. She was a member of the Republican county committee. "Solid citizen, Lieutenant. They don't come much solider."

As far as the chief of police of Cold Harbor, New York, knew, Dorothy Selby was a damn nice girl. Near the top of her graduating class at the Cold Harbor High School. Seemed to remember she'd been editor, or maybe just one of the editors, of the school annual. Gone to college for a while anyway. He didn't remember where, if he'd ever known. Went later to a secretarial school. Something like that. "Hey!"

Forniss had waited out the "Hey."

"Seems to me I heard she's been working for Arthur Jameson. Secretary or something like that. The guy who got killed yesterday. I'll be damned!"

"Yes," Charles Forniss said, "Mr. Jameson did get

killed yesterday, Chief. We're just checking around on everybody connected with him. You know how it is, Chief."

The chief of police said he sure as hell knew how it was. Charles Forniss felt, but did not express, disbelief and thanked the chief of police and hung up.

He told Heimrich this in Heimrich's office, which was as large as the office he had had at Hawthorne, where, Susan had vainly hoped, he would spend more time during more regular hours.

"All right, Charlie," Heimrich said, "we'd better go down and have a look at this meadow of the Jamesons', don't you think?"

Forniss said, "Maybe so, M.L.," and they drove southwest on US 44 in Heimrich's Buick, and on down NY 11F past The Tor's gateposts.

"This ought to be it." Forniss said, when they came to a blacktop road that branched to the left from the highway a mile or so below The Tor. They turned left onto the blacktop. For about half a mile the blacktop ran straight. Then it veered to the left and ran along a ridge—must, Heimrich thought, be running more or less parallel to the numbered highway they had quitted.

"Ought to be along here somewhere," Forniss said. "There's the house, anyway."

The Tor jutted across the valley on its high hill. The lake glittered in the morning sun. Now, as they crept along the blacktop, there was a steel mesh fence on their left. For some distance there was no break in the fence. Then there was a gap in it, with stone pillars on either side and a gate of the same steel mesh between them. The gate was closed.

"Pretty much got to be it," Forniss said, as Heimrich turned the car and headed it toward the gate, following tracks in grass. He stopped the car and Forniss got out of it. He said, "Let's hope it isn't locked," and went up to the gate. It was not locked, and Forniss pushed it open. Heimrich drove the Buick beyond the gate and stopped it, and Forniss closed the gate, which held on a catch, and got back into the car.

Ahead of them were only tracks through the stubble of a mowed field. But the tracks were clear enough. They led down steeply and then up again on a hill. Bisecting the tracks were traces of pine bark, leading away to the north and to the south, lying in the hollow between hills.

"Haying road, looks like," Heimrich said. "Seem to have hayed twice this year. The pine bark—what's left of a bridle path, wouldn't you think, Charlie?"

"Yep," Forniss said. "Looks like, M.L."

The Buick followed the tracks, down the slope, up the rise. It stopped at the top of the rise.

They looked down on the lake. It was, from this angle, long and quite narrow. Where the spit of land jutted from the opposite side to this, the meadow side, the distance was not more than a hundred and fifty yards, Heimrich thought. The boat was tied up to the pier on the far side. It bobbed innocently in the moving water. Directly across from it, below them on the meadow side, there was a similar pier of planks.

They got out of the car and followed the tracks down toward the lake. After about fifty feet, Heimrich stopped and pointed to his right. "That's the fence the horse balked, probably," he said.

The fence was of dry stone and about three feet high. There was a gap in it off to the road side. The gap was fairly wide. "For the mower and baler and trucks," Heimrich said. Beyond the fence there was a second field, also standing in stubble. It seemed to be rougher than the field they stood in. The steel fence which ran along the blacktop continued beyond the fence, cutting off the second field from trespass. It ran up a rise and disappeared over it.

"Had the stable pulled down after his wife was killed, after he sold the horses," Heimrich said. "Don't see any sign of it, do you, Charlie?"

Neither of them did. Then Forniss said, "Could have been over there," and pointed to an area near the lake where the grass still grew high and still was green; where it formed a kind of oasis in the stubble. They walked downhill toward it. They went through the tall grass and stopped.

It had once been walled with stone; some of the stone

There was a large, rectangular excavation in the grass. had fallen away from the sides and lay in the bottom of the excavation. There were daisies blooming in the excavation. They didn't, Heimrich thought, know how close winter was coming.

"Sizable stable," Heimrich said. "Did a thorough job of tearing it down, didn't they?"

The grass grew high around the excavation because the mowers had carefully avoided falling into it.

Beyond the excavation the land sloped down to the lake, which was only a hundred feet or so from it.

"Think they'd have had a drainage problem," Heimrich said. "Probably ditched it away. Handy to the boat dock, though. Thought they were going to be dragging the lake again this morning, Charlie."

Forniss said, "Yep. So did I. Could be they've finished, I suppose."

They walked down to the plank pier and out on it. Like the pier on the opposite side, this one was made of two heavy planks, supported on piles. Heimrich mentioned his guess at the distance between this pier and the other one—the one at the foot of the precipitous flight of brick stairs—to Forniss, who said, "A hundred and fifty at the most, I'd say. Take only a few minutes to row across it."

"Yes," Heimrich said. "Wonder why they didn't just row across instead of going the long way round in the Jeep? Taking the chance of getting mired on this haying road. If you can call it a road."

"Jeeps don't get mired much," Forniss said. "Maybe the old girls didn't like those damned stairs."

"Mrs. Jameson wasn't all that old," Heimrich said. "Late forties, I take it. And athletic. Liked to ride and jump her horse. Probably her sister-in-law's decision."

They walked back up the rise toward the Buick. They drove back toward the gate, and Forniss got out to open it. Heimrich got out, too, and looked back the way they had driven.

The rise in the land cut off his view of the lake and of the meadow beyond the rise. Even on a horse, he thought, Ursula Jameson could not have seen over it. Beyond the rise, Janet Jameson, even on her own horse, would have been invisible. As, of course, Ursula Jameson had said.

With the wind in the right direction, as it probably had been since the day was nice that spring of two and a half years ago, Ursula probably could have heard a horse whinny—"scream, almost. The way they sound when they're frightened." West winds bring pleasant days in the spring.

They drove the roundabout way back to The Tor.

11

On the second curve of the winding driveway up to the big house on its hill Heimrich, by stepping hard on the brake pedal, just managed not to run into the truck of Denny & Co., General Contractors. The truck stopped, too. It backed toward the side of the drive, making way— barely way—for the Buick. Heimrich drew the Buick alongside. The thin, weathered man was behind the wheel of the truck.

"Nope," he said, before Heimrich could say anything. "Not a damn thing. Not even tin cans."

"You dragged the whole lake?"

"Yeah. Like the lieutenant said to do. Who pays us?"

"The State of New York," Heimrich told him. "Send your bill to the barracks at Washington Hollow. Mark it for my attention. Heimrich. O.K.?"

The thin man said, "Yeah, I guess so," and the truck moved on down the drive. The Buick moved on up it.

156

There was a police cruiser in the turnaround, its radio talking loud. A trooper got out of it and, when he saw Heimrich, ground his cigarette out on the gravel. He said, "Sir." He said, "These men been dragging the—"

"Yes," Heimrich said, "we ran into them. Almost, anyway. Mr. Rankin's still here, I see."

What he saw was the big Chrysler. The trooper said, "Yes, sir. He's still here."

They walked up to the house and pressed the button and heard the chimes. After a minute or two, Barnes opened the door. He wore an apron to protect his dark suit. Barnes said, "Good morning, sir," with a notable lack of enthusiasm.

"We'd like a word or two with Miss Jameson," Heimrich told him.

Barnes was afraid Miss Jameson was not down yet. She was, he thought, having breakfast in her room. Mr. Jameson—it came out "Mr. Ronald"—was not down either. Rankin, however, had had breakfast and was now having coffee on the terrace. If the inspector—

"Miss Jameson," Heimrich said. "Will you ask her if she can spare us a few minutes?"

"She don't like—" Barnes said and stopped because Heimrich was shaking his head, firmly. "I'll see, sir," Barnes said, and went up the stairs.

Heimrich and Forniss went into the big drawing room. There was no fire in it now, and it was rather dark. Slivers of sunlight came in through the french doors on the south. Heimrich fished the telephone out of its retreat and dialed.

Dr. James Tennant had not regained consciousness. He had, however, been moved from the Intensive Care Ward into a private room. The surgical resident? Dr. Thompson was in surgery. Dr. Frank Wenning?

157

"I'm afraid there's no—"

"The specialist who came up from New York," Heimrich said. "To examine Dr. Tennant."

"Oh. Dr. Wenning. I'm afraid he's left the hospital, Inspector. One moment, please."

Heimrich waited the moment.

"Dr. Wenning has left, Inspector. He left quite early this morning, I'm told. To go back to New York, he told the night nurse. He's expected back here this afternoon, the nurse says."

"I'd like to be told if there is any change in Dr. Tennant's condition," Heimrich said, and gave the telephone number of The Tor. "Also, I'd like to put a man in Dr. Tennant's room so that if he—"

"That would be Administration," the Cold Harbor Hospital told him. "I'll switch you to Administration. One moment, please."

Administration, which also was female, was doubtful. The patient needed complete quiet. Even the patient's wife was not—

"A man will be along in about half an hour," Heimrich said. "He'll be a quiet man. He will just sit in the room, out of the way, and listen in case Dr. Tennant says anything. He will be in civilian clothes and entirely unobtrusive."

"Well—"

Heimrich hung up. He dialed Washington Hollow Barracks and arranged for a quiet and unobtrusive detective, in civilian clothes, to drive to Cold Harbor Hospital and sit in Dr. James Tennant's room and make notes of anything Dr. Tennant, in delirium or conscious, might say.

Heimrich went down the room and sat in a chair in front of the cold fireplace. He left the sofa for Miss Ursula Jameson, assuming she would comply with his request. Forniss sat in a chair at the other end of the sofa. They waited ten minutes, and Miss Jameson came into the room from the upper end of it. She wore a long black robe. Barnes came after her. She walked halfway down the room, her strides long. She stopped.

"It's cold in here, Barnes," she said. "And dark. Turn on some lights and start a fire."

Barnes said, "Yes, ma'am," and pressed a switch. Half a dozen lights came on in wall sconces around the long room. He went out into the entrance foyer. Miss Jameson came on down the room with the same long strides. She sat on the sofa left free for her.

"Is this never going to end?" Ursula Jameson said. "Aren't we ever to have peace?"

Heimrich and Forniss had both stood up. When Ursula was seated, Heimrich sat down again. Forniss went over to lean against the fieldstones of the fireplace.

"We're trying to find out who killed your brother, Miss Jameson," Heimrich said, his voice very low. "Once we have, we won't bother you any more."

"You've been over it and over it," she said. "I've told you over and over everything I know about it. I was asleep and—"

"And dreaming," Heimrich said. "Yes, I know. It's not about that, Miss Jameson. About something that happened more than two years ago. About Mrs. Jameson's tragic accident."

She had been looking into the lifeless fireplace. She turned, quickly, and looked at Heimrich. Her gray eyebrows went up, which gave a look of astonishment to her long-nosed face. She said, "What's that—" in a raised voice and then stopped because Heimrich was looking past her, down the room.

Barnes was coming up the room with the familiar full log carrier in his hand.

They waited while he put crumpled newspapers into the fireplace and kindling on top of the paper. He arranged logs very carefully above the kindling. He was a man precise at laying fires, and laying this one took several minutes—several minutes of silence. Finally, he used a lighter to set the newspapers afire. He stood up and watched for a moment while the kindling caught and flames began to lick up against the logs. Then he said, "Will that be all, Miss Jameson?"

"That will be all, Barnes," Ursula Jameson said, and watched the growing fire for some seconds and turned toward Heimrich. She said, "What did you ask me, Inspector?"

"We have to check back on a good many things," Heimrich said. "Things, often, which don't have anything to do with what we're actually interested in. I said we wanted to get clear what happened more than two years ago—two years ago last Memorial Day weekend. When Mrs. Jameson's horse threw her."

"I don't see what possible bearing that can have," Ursula Jameson said. "What *possible* bearing on my brother's—my brother's death."

"Probably none," Heimrich said. "Was the late Mrs. Jameson a good rider?"

"I'd always thought so. She was quite good at a good many things. Of course not—"

She stopped. Heimrich waited.

"You're asking because she was thrown," Ursula Jameson said. "Into that dreadful wall. Lots of good riders get thrown, Inspector. It's a part of—well, of what people have taken to calling the game. A chance we all take, I suppose. Didn't you know that? But then I suppose you don't ride yourself?"

It was rather more answer than Heimrich had expected. He replied to the last of it with, "Not much recently, Miss Jameson. Had Mrs. Jameson ever been thrown before, do you know?"

She shrugged wide shoulders under the black robe.

"I suppose so," she said. "I don't really know. I've had horses fall under me in my time, Inspector. With luck, you learn to land."

"As I get it," Heimrich said, "Mrs. Jameson's horse didn't fall. He just refused to jump. Do you mind telling me what you remember about the accident, Miss Jameson?"

"I told people what I knew then," she said. "Told several men several times. Don't people like you ever write things down? Things people tell you?"

"Yes," Heimrich said. "We do write things down, Miss Jameson. And I'm sorry to have to ask you to tell it all over again. I realize it must be—distressing."

"Everything is now," she said. "My brother's dead. My dear brother's—"

She stopped and put her hands over her face, covering her eyes.

"You and your sister-in-law decided to go over to the meadow and ride," Heimrich said. "It was a nice day and you'd felt cooped up. Your nephew was coming up later for the long weekend. And Dr. and Mrs. Tennant. That's what you told the trooper at the time, according to his report. The two of you were alone in the house, except for the servants—"

He stopped because Ursula Jameson had taken her hands down from her face and was shaking her head at him. He waited.

"And Miss Selby," she said. "She was in Arthur's office. I remember I could hear her typewriter."

"But your brother was in New York. To attend some dinner."

"On Fridays she types whether he's here or not," she

said. "Does over what they've done during the week, I suppose. Makes what Arthur calls—" She stopped and shook her head. "I keep forgetting," she said. "Arthur's dead. I've—I can't remember what he called it."

"A clean copy, perhaps," Heimrich said. "Miss Selby was here when you and Mrs. Jameson went off to ride?"

"I think so. I think I heard her typewriter still going. But I can't be sure. It was a long time ago. Is it important?"

"I shouldn't think so," Heimrich said. "Mrs. Jameson said she was going riding. Asked you to come along. That was the way it was?"

"Yes."

"You had Frankel row across and saddle the horses. You and Mrs. Jameson went around in the Jeep. That's what the trooper understood you to say at the time."

"That's the way it was. What difference does it make now?"

Heimrich said he was just trying to get things straight in his mind. He said that in all investigations there were likely to be ramifications. Miss Ursula Jameson made a sound which was rather like a muted snort.

"Left the Jeep near the stable, probably," Heimrich said. "Mounted. Then, Miss Jameson?"

"Rode over to the bridle path," Ursula said. "It runs along not far from the fence. Runs through a gap in the stone fence—the fence Janet's horse refused. She was riding ahead. There's room enough on the path for two to ride abreast, but she went on ahead. Then she waved and pointed and went off to the left, up the hill. Ophelia —Ophelia was my mare—wanted to go along, but I wouldn't let her. Janet rode up the hill and down on the other side—down toward the lake. It's a little hard to explain. You see—"

"We've seen the meadow," Heimrich told her. "Mrs.

162

Jameson rode up over the rise and down on the other side and out of sight from where you were. And you?"

"Just jogged along the path. Went through a gap in the fence and to the end of the far field."

"Mrs. Jameson wasn't in sight at any time?"

"No. The ridge runs the length of both fields. Anyway, I wasn't looking—trying to look. Ophelia was feeling frisky. She wanted to gallop, but I wouldn't let her. When we came back she wanted to jump the fence instead of going through the gap. She was trained as a hunter, you know."

"I didn't know," Heimrich said. "You didn't let her jump the fence?"

"My days of jumping were over years ago, Inspector. I'm an old woman. I don't need to tell you that. You can see that. An ugly old woman with nobody left."

She moved her head slowly from side to side. Her lips moved but her voice was hardly audible. "An old, old woman," he thought she said. Heimrich waited. She said, "All right. I'm sorry."

"You rode to the far side of the other field," Heimrich said. "Rode back along the bridle path. You were back about where you'd started from when you heard the other horse, Mrs. Jameson's horse. I'm just trying to get things straight in my own mind. That's the way it was?"

"Yes. I started back up the rise toward the stable. I —I thought Janet would be there waiting for me. Then I heard the horse whinny—neigh—in the way they do when they're frightened. I rode up to the top of the rise, and Alphonse—that was the name of her stallion—was —was grazing, Inspector. And Janet—it was awful, Inspector. It was—"

She broke off and again covered her eyes with her hands, as if to shutter off the memory of what she had seen.

"I know, Miss Jameson," Heimrich said. "I'm sorry to have had to put you through all this again. To make you remember things you don't want to remember. Let's see if I've got it straight."

Briefly, he went over what she had just told him, which fitted well enough with what, almost two and a half years before, she had told a State trooper. She nodded her head in agreement with his summary. Yes, she was almost sure that Dorothy Selby had been in the house, at her typewriter, when she and Janet had left it in the Jeep. Yes, her nephew Ronald had been at The Tor when she drove back to it in the Jeep, having decided that there was nothing she could do for Janet. "Nothing anybody could do for her."

"After that—well, after that it's all confused. Vague. They told me afterward that I fainted, or almost fainted. That I was—that I was talking without making sense. I don't remember, Inspector."

"Naturally," Heimrich said. "It was a very shocking thing for you, Miss Jameson. Ronald Jameson was here when you got back. Dr. and Mrs. Tennant came a little later. That's the way it was?"

"I guess so. They must have, I suppose. It's all—all mixed up in my mind."

"Of course," Heimrich said. "There's just one other small point, Miss Jameson. Then I'll quit bothering you for now."

"I don't see what all this has to do with—with Arthur's death. What point, Inspector?"

"From the time Mrs. Jameson left the path and rode up the hill," Heimrich said, "about how long was it before you heard her horse neighing? Or, as you told the trooper at the time, almost screaming? And rode up the rise on your horse to see whether something had happened?"

"I don't know. Oh, half an hour perhaps. Perhaps a little longer than that."

"You didn't keep track of the time? Because, I suppose, you and Mrs. Jameson wanted to be back here by the time your guests arrived."

"Wait," she said. "I do remember. It was a long time ago, but I do remember. Because I thought of that—of Ronald and the Tennants coming up for the weekend—and looked at my watch. Half an hour at least before I heard Alphonse. Perhaps three quarters of an hour. I remember thinking it was time we got back."

"And during that half an hour, or forty-five minutes perhaps, Mrs. Jameson was out of your sight?"

"Behind the rise. I told you that."

"Yes," Heimrich said. "I think I've got it all clear in my mind now. I'm sorry to have had to bother you this way."

"I suppose you have to," she said. "I don't know why, but I suppose you have to. You're going now, then?"

"Not quite yet," Heimrich said. "By the way, can you tell me what Mrs. Jameson looked like?"

"Her portrait's up there," she said, and pointed toward the upper end of the long room. "He had portraits painted of both of them."

Heimrich nodded his head. He said, "Your nephew is still around, I take it? I'd like a few words with him. Be all right if I have Barnes or somebody ask him to come down?"

"I'm going up," Ursula Jameson said. "If this—this interrogation is over?"

"Quite over, Miss Jameson."

"I'll tell Ronald you want to see him," she said, and stood up and walked away from the fire and up the long room. She did not, Merton Heimrich thought again, walk like an old woman. She went out of the room.

165

After a minute or so, Heimrich got up himself and walked up the room.

The portrait of Janet Jameson was in a heavy gold frame, like that of the portrait of Rebecca Jameson on the wall between the french doors. There was no resemblance between Arthur Jameson's two wives, except that both of them had been beautiful. (Or, perhaps, made so by the painters who had done portraits of them. Heimrich thought that perhaps one painter had done both portraits. It seemed to him that there was a similarity in method. On the other hand, they would have been done at least twenty years apart. Susan would know, he thought. I can only guess.)

Janet Jameson did not look to be past forty-five. Probably had not been when she sat for her portrait. Or, as it appeared, stood for it—stood in an evening dress which left her shoulders, and a considerable area of her breasts, bare. She had been tall and slender, unless a painter had been extremely flattering. She had had dark hair which fell to the bare shoulders. She had had blue eyes and a short, shapely nose. Her mouth had been a little large and was shaped in a smile—a warm and somehow glowing smile. When she had been painted she had been, at a guess, in her late twenties—possibly early thirties. But portrait painters can take years off of ages. (Or, of course, add years to them, if they choose. Heimrich did not suppose that they often chose so. Subjects are also customers.)

He went back to the fire, which was leaping. It was too warm in front of the fire; the room had been warm when Ursula Jameson had come into it and found it cold. Forniss had left the fireplace and gone to stand near one of the french doors. Heimrich went to stand beside him.

"Five minutes at the outside to row to this side,"

Forniss said. "And the fence is maybe two, three hundred yards from the stable."

"Yes," Heimrich said, and joined Forniss in looking through the net-covered glass of the french door. Geoffrey Rankin was sitting in a chaise at the far end of the terrace. A small table beside him held a silver coffee pot and a cup. Rankin was smoking a cigarette and reading a newspaper, which Heimrich took to be the New York Times. He was wearing a tweed jacket and what looked like heavyweight gray slacks. He was sitting in the sun and in a sheltered spot.

"Aunt Ursula says you want to see me." The voice behind Heimrich and Forniss was heavy. Ronald Jameson hadn't lost any weight either, and his black hair still bristled. This morning, Heimrich thought, Jameson looked a little younger than he had the day before. He wore a dark blue polo shirt. He did not bulge anywhere beneath the blue shirt. In his late forties or early fifties, Ronald Jameson was keeping his figure. He would never have the slender grace his father had had, but he had a symmetry of his own.

He was not wearing a jacket.

"The old girl keeps it damn hot in this house," Ronald Jameson said. "Always has. Always did, anyway, when I was around as a kid. What do you want to see me about, Inspector? Something about Jan's accident, my aunt says. She can't think why. Neither can I, come to that."

"We like to get everything clear," Heimrich said. "Way it's laid down in the rules, you know."

Ronald Jameson said, "Yeah?" and put a good deal of skepticism into the word.

Heimrich ignored the intonation. He said, "Yes. Waste a lot of time, probably. Maybe we could sit down some place? Over there?"

167

He gestured toward the sofa in front of the fire.

"Too damn hot," Jameson said. "Terrace, maybe?"

"Rankin's on the terrace," Heimrich said. "Reading the newspaper. I don't think we want to interrupt him, Mr. Jameson."

Jameson went over to the window and looked out at Geoffrey Rankin. He turned back to Heimrich.

"He's getting edgy as hell about being cooped up here," Jameson said. "So'm I, come to that. I had a conference this morning and had to phone and call it off. How long are you going to keep us hanging around, huh? And by the way, how's Jim Tennant doing, or don't you know?"

"No longer than I have to," Heimrich said. "Dr. Tennant is still unconscious. We can talk here, if you like. Only we'd be more comfortable sitting down, wouldn't we? Not that it will take very long."

"All right," Jameson said. "We can go up to my room, I guess. At least I've got the windows open and this damned heat off."

They went up the wide staircase from the entrance foyer and along a corridor and into a corner room on the second floor. The windows were open, all right.

There was a wide double bed along one wall, spread up. There were several chairs and a big chest of drawers. Jameson's suitcase stood near the door to the corridor.

"All packed and ready to go," Jameson said. "All right. Sit down, the two of you, and shoot."

He sat down himself, taking a chair in the cross breeze between two windows. It was evident that Ronald Jameson did not mind sitting in a draft.

"Miss Jameson told you we were asking about your stepmother's accident," Heimrich said. "And I know it was a long time ago and probably hasn't any connection with Mr. Jameson's death. However—"

168

"What do you mean, probably?"

"Just that," Heimrich told him. "Miss Jameson came back here in the Jeep after she found Mrs. Jameson dead with her head bashed in against the stone fence. Found you already here. That's right?"

"Yes."

"Miss Jameson was very shaken up, of course. Almost hysterical, as she remembers it. Fainted, she thinks. Way you remember it?"

"She came racketing up in the Jeep," Jameson said. "Skidded all over the drive when she stopped it. I'd just got here. Just gone into the house. I ran out when I heard the racket and she—well, she came damn near falling out of the Jeep. She was screaming. Over and over she kept saying 'Janet's. Janet's.' That's all I could get out of her at first—just something about Jan. As if something had happened to Jan. I took her inside and for quite a while I couldn't get anything else out of her. Finally she said, 'Dead. Jan's dead. That awful horse.' Something like that."

"And she fainted?"

"Seemed about to. I got one of the maids to take care of her. Nobody who's here now. The servants Aunt Ursula had then—well, they quit afterward. After Jan got killed that way. Thought there was a curse on the place or something, I guess. This maid—I don't remember her name—finally got Aunt Ursula up to bed. Anyway, she was upstairs when I—when I got back."

"Back, Mr. Jameson?"

"From what Aunt Ursula said, about the 'awful' horse and all, I figured Jan had had an accident. I called the police and, I think, for an ambulance. Then I got in the Jeep—she'd left the motor running—and drove around to the meadow. To where they must have been riding. Aunt Ursula was dressed for riding. Did I tell you that?"

"No, you hadn't. You drove around the long way. Instead of rowing across, which might have been quicker."

"Sure. My aunt did say that Jan was dead. But, hell, you can't always tell. She might just have been hurt. With the Jeep I could—well, I could have brought her back here. I'd told—I think I'd told—the ambulance to come here. Also, I'm pretty sure I'd called the doctor. It was all pretty mixed up, Inspector. And, as you said, it was quite a long time ago."

"Yes, Mr. Jameson. You drove around to the meadow. As far as the fence, I suppose?"

"I must have—yes. Past the stable. Saw Aunt Ursula's mare loose. Grazing. And the other horse the same, only farther along. Saddled and grazing. Then—well, then I saw Jan lying with her head against this damned stone fence. And saw that Aunt Ursula was right. Had to be right. It was—well, it was a damned bad thing to see. Maybe people like you get used to seeing anything."

"No," Heimrich said, "it doesn't get to be like that. Her head was—I gather it was crushed against the wall."

"Damn it," Jameson said, "do you have to make me see it again?" His low, heavy voice shook a little. Then, almost as if to himself, he said, "She was so damned pretty. So damned—" He stopped, and shook his head. "She wasn't even as old as I was, you know. Stepmother or not. She—" Again he stopped. Then he said, "There's a portrait of her downstairs. Maybe you saw it?"

"Yes. She was a beautiful woman."

"Makes her look taller than she was really—but pretty, anyway. Damned pretty. Until—strange thing is, her face wasn't damaged much. Just her head. All smashed in and—damn it to hell. *Damn it to hell.*" His heavy voice shook again on the words.

"A bad thing to see," Heimrich said. "A bad thing to

remember. I'm sorry, Mr. Jameson. You were fond of her, probably?"

For some seconds, Ronald Jameson merely looked down at the floor. He seemed to be staring at the yellow rug on the floor. He said, again as if to himself, "You could call it that." Then, abruptly, he looked up at Heimrich. When he spoke his voice was heavy. It was also grating. "You mean something by that?" he said.

Heimrich shook his head. He said, "Just that I assume you were fond of her, Mr. Jameson. From the way you speak of her. That's all I meant."

"It was an awful thing to see. It would have been an awful thing to look at if—hell, if she'd been somebody I'd never seen before. Can't you get that through your head?"

"Yes. I can get that through my head, Mr. Jameson."

"I liked Jan, sure. If you want to say I was fond of her, all right. Also, she was my father's wife."

"Of course," Heimrich said. "I didn't mean what you seem to think I meant, Mr. Jameson. Your father's wife, of course. A great deal younger than your father, as it happened. Younger even than you, you say. Were you here often then, Mr. Jameson? When your stepmother was still alive?"

"Not often. Oh, now and then."

"More often than in the last couple of years?"

"Maybe. Not to see Jan, if that's what you're getting at. Is that what you're getting at?"

"Not at anything," Heimrich said. "Just trying to get things clear in my mind."

He was getting rather tired of hearing himself say that.

"And thanks for helping me," he added. "I'm sorry to have to put you through this. Bring back things you —anybody—would rather forget."

"I can't see what good it's done you," Jameson said.

"Just—just raking things up, aren't you? To—to what? To prove you're a hell of a good detective?"

There was definite rancor in his voice now.

"Probably it's not done me any good," Heimrich said. "I'm supposed to find out what I can is all. Sorry if I've upset you. Just a couple of other things. Was Miss Selby still here that afternoon, do you know?"

"Father was in town," Jameson said. "Why'd she be here?"

"Your aunt thinks she was. Making a clean copy of work she and your father had done during the week. Typing out notes, possibly. You didn't see her?"

"No. And that beat-up Volks of hers wasn't around. If she'd been here she'd gone by the time I got here. Which was just before Aunt Ursula came charging up in the Jeep and pretty much fell out of it. I told you that."

"Yes," Heimrich said. "You did tell me that. When you found Mrs. Jameson dead was the ground torn up on the near side of the fence? Where this stallion of hers had balked the jump? Dug his hooves in, I'd think. Made—oh, furrows in the turf?"

"Look, all I saw was Jan with her head smashed in. You think I was in a shape to look at anything else?"

"I wouldn't have been," Heimrich said. Which of course was not true; it is a professional need to try to see everything. "Do you happen to know whether photographs were taken? Before—I suppose the ambulance went down there? And, probably, there was a good deal of tramping around while they were getting Mrs. Jameson into the ambulance."

"Getting her body in," Jameson said. "No, I don't remember anybody's taking photographs, if that's what you mean. It was—well, it was a pretty obvious accident. You trying to say it wasn't?"

"I'm not trying to say anything," Heimrich told the

heavy, now glowering, man. "Just trying to find out about things." He stood up and Forniss stood up. "Sorry if I've given you a bad time," Heimrich said. "Lieutenant Forniss and I'll be getting along now."

Jameson got up slowly from his chair.

"All right," he said. "I suppose you've got to do what you think's your job."

There was no cordiality in his voice.

Heimrich and Forniss went down the wide staircase. There was nobody in the entrance foyer, or in the long living room. Forniss said, "Rankin?"

"I don't think so, Charlie," Heimrich said. "Not now, anyway. I think the girl, don't you? And Frankel."

He got into the Buick. Forniss did not. He said, "O.K.—Frankel." Heimrich started the engine. Forniss said, "I suppose we're thinking the same thing, M.L.?"

"Probably," Heimrich said. "Wondering about the same thing, anyway."

"Half an hour," Forniss said. "Maybe forty-five minutes. A long time to gallop across half a field and get thrown into a stone wall."

"Yes," Heimrich said. "We're thinking pretty much the same thing. Meet you at the Inn, Charlie."

In Cold Harbor Heimrich turned the Buick into Vine Street and drove up it.

12

Frans Frankel was not in the apartment above the garage. Forniss had to wait for a minute or two for Mrs. Frankel to come to the door and tell him that. First she said, "You again."

"He's working," she said. "He's got work to do. So've I."

"We all have work to do," Forniss said. "Where'll I find your husband, Mrs. Frankel?"

"In the garden, where else?" she said. She started to close the door. Forniss said, "Where's the garden, Mrs. Frankel?"

"Other side of the house, where else?" Mrs. Frankel said, and closed the door firmly.

Forniss walked back to the house and around it. A hundred yards or so north of the house, a little lower down the hill, bordered by a low, taut, chicken-wire fence, was a leveled area of roughly two hundred by four hundred feet. It was bisected by a path of pine bark.

Frans Frankel was a big man in worn slacks with dirt on the knees of them. He was digging something out of the ground—something set in rows. Forniss stepped over the fence. Frankel turned to look at him and then thrust a spading fork into the soil. He'll say, "You again," Forniss thought. Frankel said, "Morning, Lieutenant. We got a frost last night. Got to clean up for winter."

He forked a bulb out of the soil. He lifted the still-green blades to which it was attached and shook it and earth fell away from the bulb. He tossed vigorously and the bulb and the blades flew over the fence to join others lying in a heap on grass in the sun.

"Glads won't winter over up here," Frankel said. "You wanted to see me, Lieutenant? Already told you all I know."

He thrust the spading fork again into the soil and wiggled it and bent to grasp the blades of another glad bulb.

"About something else," Forniss said. "Think maybe you can help us."

Frankel said "Uh" and shook earth from another glad bulb and tossed it over the fence.

"Couple of years ago," Forniss said, "Mrs. Jameson got killed in an accident. More than two years ago. Her horse threw her into a stone wall."

Frankel said, "Yeah." His tone was flat. He thrust the fork into the soil again, but this time he turned from it and faced Forniss. He said, "Crazy damn horse. She was a nice little lady."

"From what we hear," Forniss said, "Miss Jameson asked you to row across the lake and saddle the horses. So that she and Mrs. Jameson could go around in the Jeep. That's the way it was?"

"Yeah. That's what she told me, so that's what I did. Rowed over and rowed back. I was planting glads. Like these I'm digging up. They was right pretty in July."

"You went over and saddled the horses." Forniss said. "When you came back, did you see Miss Jameson and her sister-in-law?"

"No. Went around the back way. Shorter."

"You didn't see them drive off in the Jeep?"

"Can't say I did. Couldn't, the way I came back here. To get the bulbs in."

"You didn't stop by to tell them the horses were ready?"

"No. Been no point to it, would there? She knows when I've got a job to do I do it. Wanted to get the glads in before I knocked off."

He prized another bulb clump out of the soil. This time two bulbs came with the blades.

"About what time was this?" Forniss asked him.

"Maybe four. Maybe a little after."

"Did you hear the Jeep when it started up? I suppose Miss Jameson would have been driving it?"

"No. House in between. And I was down on my knees putting bulbs in. Sure she'd have been driving it."

"About how long did it take you to row across, saddle the horses and row back and tie up the boat?"

"Maybe twenty minutes. Maybe half an hour. You think I keep looking at my watch?"

"So you were back at, say, about four-thirty?"

"About then, I'd guess."

"They might have driven off in the Jeep while you were over on the other side of the lake?"

"Sure. They hadn't got around when I tied the horses up, though."

"Or," Forniss said, "they might not have gone until after you came back?"

"Sure."

"This was on a Friday? The twenty-ninth of May? Since Memorial Day fell on a Saturday that year, the holiday was the following Monday?"

"If you say so," Frankel said, and thrust the spading fork into the soil beside another glad plant and prized another bulb out of the earth.

"Way we get it," Forniss said, "Miss Selby was here that day—that Friday. Working in Mr. Jameson's office, although Mr. Jameson himself was in New York. Way you remember it, Mr. Frankel?"

Frankel shook earth from the newly excavated glad bulb and threw it over the fence to join the others.

"Don't remember it one way or the other," Frankel said, and pushed the fork back into the earth. "Usually here on Fridays, I guess. See her Volks out in front of the house." He left the fork sticking upright in the earth and turned to Forniss.

"What goes on in the house ain't much concern to us," he said. "To me and Gretchen. Now and then she goes over and helps out in the house. Special like. I take care of the grounds and do outside work. Call it caretaker if you want to. Or 'yardman,' way she does."

"She?"

"Miss Jameson, who else? Thing is, they've got people working in the house. What she calls the staff. Nothing to do with Gretchen and me 'cept when she asks her to help out."

Forniss said he saw. He thought that he wasn't getting much of any place and that Frankel was rather going out of his way to make it clear that he and his wife weren't servants at The Tor.

"All the inside people quit after Mrs. Jameson got herself killed," Frankel said. "Not that Miss Jameson wasn't running things before that. Has been as long as we've been here."

"How long's that been, Mr. Frankel?"

"Five years. More like six, I guess."

"Then you and Mrs. Frankel weren't here when the first Mrs. Jameson was alive?"

"No. I was running the greenhouse then. Place my father used to own, if you want to know."

Forniss didn't especially want to know.

"By the way," Forniss said, "was Mrs. Frankel in the apartment that afternoon, do you happen to remember? You can see the turnaround from the apartment windows, reason I'm asking."

"This was a Friday from what you say. Fridays the wife does her marketing. For the weekend."

"You and your wife have your own car, I suppose? I mean, she can drive herself in to do the marketing."

"Sure do. What'd you think?"

Frankel turned back to his spading fork and dug up another glad bulb and shook it and tossed it over the fence. Forniss said, "Thanks, Mr. Frankel," and thought it was thanks for nothing and stepped back over the fence. He walked back up to the house and across the turnaround, past the terrace and the path which led from it to the top of the steep brick staircase. He climbed the stairs to the apartment above the garage and rang the doorbell and waited for a minute or two. Mrs. Frankel came to the door, carrying a mop. She said, as he expected, "You again. Couldn't you find him?"

"Yes, I found Mr. Frankel," Forniss said. "You remember the day Mrs. Jameson was killed, Mrs. Frankel? Thrown from her horse?"

"Of course I do. Bad thing. She was such a pretty little lady."

"We're trying to check up on times," Forniss said. "When Mrs. Jameson and her sister-in-law drove over to the meadow to ride their horses. You can see the space in front of the house from your windows here. Just wondered if you happened to see the Jeep start off and can help us about what time it was."

"I was in Cold Harbor marketing," Mrs. Frankel said.

178

"So how could I see when they started over to this meadow? All over when I got back. Poor little thing."

"Mrs. Jameson," Forniss said. "Yes. You've twice said she was little. So did your husband."

"Couldn't have weighed more than a hundred pounds. Skin and bones I'd call it. For all she was always doing things. Like riding horses and playing tennis and all. And swimming in that lake of theirs, for all she shouldn't have ought to."

"Shouldn't have ought to?"

"Drains into a water supply," Mrs. Frankel said. "Some law about it. Think you'd know that, being a policeman."

Forniss said, "Thank you, Mrs. Frankel. Sorry to have interrupted your work."

He got "Huh!" and an abruptly closed door and went back down the stairs.

Not more than a hundred pounds, Forniss thought. Not too heavy a burden for a strong man. Or, for that matter, a strong woman. He looked at his watch. It was a little after eleven. Too early to meet M.L. at the Old Stone Inn in Van Brunt. He hoped M.L. was getting more than he was and walked back toward the house.

Geoffrey Rankin was still sitting in the sun on the terrace. He wasn't reading a newspaper, and there was a glass instead of a coffee cup on the table beside his chaise. Forniss walked up onto the terrace and said, "Good morning, Mr. Rankin."

"You," Rankin said. "How long are you guys going to keep me here?"

"We're not keeping you," Forniss said. "The inspector told you that." He pulled a chair up and sat on it.

"The hell you're not," Rankin said. "I can't stir without one of your men on my tail. I went over to see Miss Selby because I couldn't get her on the phone. Damn

179

line was busy for hours, then the operator said it was out of order. So I got in my car and took off. But what if I hadn't come back here?"

"You wouldn't have been stopped, wherever you went. Those were the inspector's orders."

"Just followed," Rankin said. "Got a cigarette on you?"

Forniss held out a pack toward Rankin. After Rankin had shaken a cigarette out of it, Forniss pulled one out for himself. They both lighted cigarettes.

"So," Rankin said, "are you getting anywhere? Finding out who killed the old boy?"

"We will," Forniss said. "By the way, way I get it you'd not been here before. Not until the party Saturday night, when Miss Selby showed you the way up. That's right?"

"That's right. And I'd never seen Arthur Jameson until he put on that god-awful show. Just heard about him."

"From Miss Selby, I suppose?"

"Yes. Distinguished old gentleman, she called him. Distinguished old—"

He stopped himself. Forniss gave him time, which he did not use.

"So you couldn't have been here—here at The Tor— on the Friday before Memorial Day a couple of years ago?"

"I sure as hell wasn't. Wait a minute. That was the day Mrs. Jameson fell off her horse, wasn't it? Don't tell me you're prying into that, Forniss. Why the hell would you?"

"No special reason I know of," Forniss said. "Inspector Heimrich gets curious about things. I suppose Miss Selby told you about Mrs. Jameson's accident?"

"Do you? Maybe she did. Also, it was in the papers. Read the *Times* this morning?"

"Glanced at it," Forniss said.

"Front page," Rankin said. "Mysterious death of member of a distinguished Hudson River family. State police are investigating—"

"Yes," Forniss said, and drew on his cigarette.

"Mrs. Arthur Jameson dies in riding accident," Rankin said. "Wife of a member of long-established Hudson Valley family. Something like that two years ago."

"You seem to have kept up with the Jameson family," Forniss said. He paused to draw again on his cigarette and let smoke drift from his mouth. The wind caught the smoke and the smoke vanished. "Why is that, Mr. Rankin? Because Miss Selby worked for Mr. Jameson? As a matter of fact, she was here in the house the day Mrs. Jameson was killed."

The cigarette had burned down. He stubbed it out. I smoke too fast, Forniss thought. Rankin has had only a couple of drags from his. In fact, Rankin has let his cigarette go out.

"Did she tell you that, Mr. Rankin?" Forniss asked.

"Any reason she should have?"

Forniss shrugged his shoulders.

"Just thought she might have mentioned it," Forniss said. "Sort of thing people'd talk about, I'd think. 'Dreadful thing about poor Mrs. Jameson. And I was right there in their house when it happened.' That sort of thing."

"Maybe she did. Dot and I haven't seen much of each other the last couple of years. As I told the inspector."

"Sure you did," Forniss said. "I forget things, I guess. Before that—before she went to work as Mr. Jameson's secretary—you saw quite a bit of each other. Or don't I remember that right, either?"

"We saw a bit of each other, yes. There was no secret about it."

"No reason there should have been, I'd think," Forniss

said. "You and she being related and all. Distantly re-lated, that is. Not—how was it you put it, Mr. Rankin? Within the bounds of con-something?"

"Consanguinity," Rankin said. "Kinship. In our case not anywhere near close enough to—" He stopped. Then he said, "Getting at something, Lieutenant?"

"I think you're getting at it, Mr. Rankin. A pretty young woman, as you pointed out. Only a few years younger than you. A great many years younger than the man she was engaged to. A girl you seem to have stopped seeing about the time she came here to work with Mr. Jameson. Any objection to telling me why you and she stopped seeing each other?"

"Yes," Rankin said. "And it's none of your damn business, is it?"

Forniss lighted another cigarette before he answered. This sort of thing was causing him to step up his smoking when he was trying to step it down. When he spoke, he spoke very slowly.

"Mr. Rankin," Forniss said, "I'm a detective working on a murder case. Anything related to that case, even remotely, is my business. Miss Selby was engaged to Arthur Jameson. A couple of years back you and Miss Selby saw a good deal of each other. Rather suddenly, I gather, you pretty much stopped seeing each other. All I asked you was why."

"What you're hinting at," Rankin said, and he, too, spoke slowly, "is that I'm in love with Dot and killed the old boy so he couldn't marry her. That we stopped seeing each other because she was going to work for Jameson. Which, Forniss, is a lot of bull."

Forniss said, "All right, Mr. Rankin." But he did not make any move to get up from his chair. He merely looked at Rankin and waited, as if he expected Rankin

182

to go on with something, to finish something. Sometimes it works.

"So you're way off base," Rankin said.

"All right."

"It was that mother of hers," Rankin said. "She—all right. She wanted to break it up. Not that there was anything to break up. Said it wouldn't be seemly. That Flo—well, she gets ideas into that head of hers. Crazy ideas. About genes. About which she doesn't know a damn thing, actually."

"About genes, Mr. Rankin?"

"Old wives' tales. Men and women who are related even as distantly as Dot and I are shouldn't have anything to do with each other. Never heard of the royal families of Europe, apparently. Trouble with Dot, she believes what Mama tells her. Believes—well, believes all the taboos. Even makes them up herself. Flo, I mean."

"That was the—" Forniss began and stopped because Rankin was not listening; was ready to go on. You never stop a witness who wants to talk.

"Having short little fingers on the left hand runs in a family," Rankin said. "If even distant blood relations in that family marry and have children, the children won't have left arms. See anything the matter with my hands, Forniss?"

He held his hands up, the fingers spread apart. There wasn't anything the matter with his hands.

"All right," Forniss said. "And I've seen Miss Selby's hands. When she was shooting arrows at a target, incidentally. Very good-looking hands, hers are. You're going a long way around something, aren't you?"

"Ever hear about the wharf cats in New York, Forniss? Kill the wharf rats for a living. And inbreed like crazy.

And keep on getting bigger and tougher and killing more rats."

"I've heard about them," Forniss said. "Apparently you've given this thing about inbreeding a good deal of thought, Mr. Rankin. Because of this very distant relationship between you and Miss Selby. Which makes it pretty obvious, doesn't it?"

As he had talked on, Rankin had been looking not at Forniss but across the closely mowed lawn—had been, in fact, looking in the direction of the top of the brick staircase which plunged down toward the lake. Now he looked at Forniss, and his eyes narrowed.

"Makes what obvious?" Rankin said.

"Oh," Forniss said, "that you and Miss Selby were, at one time anyway, a good deal more than the casual acquaintances you've been telling us. That you wanted to marry her and that her mother scared her off. Made her believe you were too close kin to marry."

"Which we damn well aren't."

"All right."

"Hell, Eleanor and Franklin Roosevelt had the same great, great—I don't know how many greats to put in—grandfather. So what?"

"So nothing," Forniss said. "I'm not agreeing with Florence Selby, Mr. Rankin. The point is, apparently, that she persuaded her daughter. You did want to marry Dorothy Selby. Isn't that right? Do now, at a guess."

"What you guess isn't—"

"I know," Forniss said. "Isn't evidence. You told us Miss Selby asked you, relaying a message from the Jamesons, of course, to come up to this party Saturday night. That you accepted, thinking it was just a birthday party for a man she worked with. That nobody told you it was also a celebration of her engagement to

Jameson. Must have come as something of a shock to you, Mr. Rankin."

Again, Geoffrey Rankin looked away across the lawn. He said nothing for several seconds. Then he said, "Got another cigarette? I seem to have let this one go out."

Forniss had another cigarette to give to Rankin. Rankin lighted the cigarette.

"All right," he said. "It was a bitchy thing for her to do. There's a little bitchiness in all of them, isn't there? Even in the best of them."

"There's a little bitchiness in all of us," Forniss said. "It isn't limited to women."

He stood up.

"And," Rankin said, "I didn't kill the old boy to keep him from marrying Dot."

"All right, Mr. Rankin," Forniss said, and walked off the terrace toward the turnaround, in which the police cruiser was standing, its motor dead but its radio chattering. As he walked, he looked at his watch. Eleven-forty. Still too early to meet M.L. at the Old Stone Inn at Van Brunt. Still—

"Your sidekick in the house?" Forniss asked the trooper.

The trooper returned, with a visible start, from wherever he had been. He said, "Yes, sir, Lieutenant. We were told to stick around. Just to see nobody—"

"Yes," Forniss said, and went around the car and got in beside the trooper. "You can run me in to the Inn in Van Brunt. Your sidekick can see that nobody gets away."

The trooper said, "Sir," and started the motor.

Of course, Charles Forniss thought as they went south on NY 11F, Rankin merely confirmed what we'd already guessed.

It was still too early for the lunch customers to have showed up at the Old Stone Inn. Not that there would be many on Monday. On the other hand, on Mondays the bar didn't have to wait until one in the afternoon to open.

Heimrich was not in the taproom. Neither was anybody else, except the new man behind the bar. He was reading the New York *Daily News*. He put the *News* under the bar when Forniss walked up to it and said, "Good morning, sir."

* * * *

"Mother isn't here," Dorothy Selby had said when she opened the door of the house on Vine Street. "Is it Mother you want to see? Because she's out with prospects, I think. Did you try the office, Inspector?"

"No," Heimrich said. "Perhaps you can spare me a few minutes yourself, Miss Selby? Help me get one or two points straight in my head?"

She said, "Of course, Inspector," and he followed her into the big living room.

She was much more composed today than she had been the day before, Heimrich thought. The shock of her fiancé's death appeared to have worn off. Rather quickly, Heimrich thought, and thought that the young are resilient. She looked very young in a short skirt and a sleeveless blouse. She had very pretty legs. She had applied lipstick expertly. She did not look as if she had planned to spend the day alone in the house. Expecting a visitor? The same visitor she had had the day before?

"Just trying to clear up a couple of points," Heimrich said. "Think maybe you can help. Not about Mr. Jameson's death, directly."

Momentarily, she closed her eyes. They were large

186

blue eyes. Her blond hair curved softly down to her shoulders. She opened her eyes.

"I want to help in any way I can," she said.

"I'd like you to remember back," Heimrich said. "Back more than two years. You were working with Mr. Jameson then?"

"For him. Yes."

"The Friday before Memorial Day two years ago," Heimrich said.

"The day Janet was killed. In that awful accident. No, Inspector, I'll never forget that day."

"From what we hear, you were at the Jameson house that afternoon. In Mr. Jameson's study, working."

"His office. Arthur always called it his office. Yes, I was there, Inspector. Making a clean copy of what we'd done during the week. On the book, I mean."

"About when did you leave that afternoon?"

"Somewhere around four, I think."

"Had Miss Jameson and her sister-in-law driven over to the meadow when you left, do you remember?"

She was silent for a moment. Then she shook her head.

"I don't think I saw either of them at all that day," she said. "I think I got there—oh, around ten that morning. Went directly to the office without seeing anyone. I had my own house key. Miss Jameson gave one to me when I first went there to help Arthur. But I don't think the door was locked that morning. Anyway, I went to the office and began to type. Around one o'clock the man they had then—it wasn't Barnes then: I don't remember the man's name—anyway, he brought me in sandwiches and coffee. Then I went back to work."

"Until around four," Heimrich said. "Did the others in the house know you were there, do you think? Aside from the man who brought you your lunch, I mean?"

"I don't know. Oh, probably they heard the type-writer going."

"You went out of the house about four," Heimrich said. "Was the Jeep in front of the house, do you remember? The one they drove in to the meadow. After Frankel had saddled up their horses."

She closed her eyes again, as if she were trying to remember. Then, slowly, she nodded her head.

"I think so," she said. "I think I remember its being there. Headed toward the drive, I think."

"The motor running?"

She didn't remember about that. Anyway, she didn't remember that it was. Then she said, "Wait a minute." She opened her eyes again.

"I said I didn't see Miss Jameson or Janet that day," she said. "I just remembered. I was in my car and starting toward the driveway when they came out of the house. Dressed for riding. I saw them in the rearview mirror." She paused. She said, "Why all this, Inspector? I don't understand."

It had taken her, Heimrich thought, some time to get around to the obvious question. He told her he was just trying to get things straight in his mind.

"When they came out," Heimrich said. "Dressed for riding. Did they go over and get in the Jeep?"

She shook her head.

"I don't know," Dorothy Selby said. "I just saw them come out of the house. Then I'd gone around the curve at the top of the driveway and couldn't see them any more."

Heimrich said he saw.

"Just the Jeep in the turnaround?" He said. "No other car?"

"I don't remember any other car."

188

"Mr. Jameson—Mr. Ronald Jameson, I mean—hadn't got there yet? Apparently he did come up a little later. Was there, anyway, when Miss Jameson drove back to tell what had happened."

"I don't know," she said. "His car wasn't in front of the house. But then, if he was going to be there overnight, he always put the car in the garage. He's sort of—oh, old-maidish—about that car of his. It's a Mercedes, you know. Like Mother's. Not an old rattletrap like mine."

Heimrich said, "Yes," which didn't mean much of anything. He said, "Speaking of cars, Miss Selby. Mr. Rankin drove over here to see you yesterday."

"And you had him followed," she said. "He knew it. Did you know he knew it?"

"Yes. He told us he saw the police car. What did he come to see you about, Miss Selby?"

She said, "About?" Then she said, "Oh, to see if I was all right. To—to tell me how sorry he was."

"Considerate of him."

"Of course. That's the way he is. And after all we're—we're relations. Cousins. Didn't we tell you that?"

"Very distant cousins," Heimrich said. "Yes, you've told us that. Not at all a close degree of relationship. He drove over to—call it make a sympathy call—because you and he are distant relatives?"

"Of course. Oh, we were friends, too. Some time ago he used to take me places. In the city, mostly."

"Because you were what you call cousins?"

"Of course. What else could it have been?"

He merely looked at her, and let her see that he was looking at her. He thought she was intelligent enough not to need words for it.

"No," she said. "It wasn't like that at all. How could

it have been? We are cousins. And Mother made me see—" She stopped abruptly. Heimrich waited.

"Nothing," she said. "I wasn't going to say anything."

Heimrich nodded his head acceptingly.

"When Mr. Rankin came up here from town Saturday night," he said. "When you guided him over to the Jameson place, having passed along their invitation—he thought the party was just a birthday celebration?"

"Yes. I guess so, anyway. I hadn't—" Again she stopped without finishing the sentence.

"So when Mr. Jameson announced that you and he were going to get married, it must have come as a surprise to Mr. Rankin?"

"I hadn't told him about it, if that's what you mean. He was a little late in getting here that night, and I went right off in the Volks and he followed me. We didn't—didn't stand around talking. He didn't even get out of his car."

"At the party you did. You didn't tell him then you were going to marry Jameson? Before Jameson made that—that announcement of his?"

"I didn't want him to," she said. "Not that way. It—it seemed a very old-fashioned way. Rather—oh, I don't know. Theatrical? You were there, weren't you? At the party?"

"Yes," Heimrich said. "So it came as a surprise to Mr. Rankin. As far as you know, anyway. An unpleasant surprise, Miss Selby? Even, perhaps. a rather shattering surprise?"

She said she did not know what he meant. She said, " 'Shattering,' Inspector? What a strange word to use. As if—" Again she did not finish.

"Yes," Heimrich said. "As if he were shocked by what you were going to do."

She shook her head in bewilderment. Or a simulation of bewilderment?

"Why should he have been, Inspector? I told you we were—we are—friends. Jeff—why, Jeff would want me to be happy." She paused. "And we *would* have been happy, Arthur and I. You talk as if—you talk as if you think there was something between Jeff and me. We were just friends. I keep telling you that. Friends and relatives. Anything else would have been—would have been impossible. Surely you—

She stopped, this time because Heimrich was slowly shaking his head.

"No," he said. "Not impossible, Miss Selby. And yes, I do think there was something more between the two of you than casual friendship and distant relationship."

She had been relaxed in her chair until then. Then her slim body stiffened. She grasped both arms of the chair, as if she were about to pull herself out of it. Her lips began to move, but for seconds no words came from them. Finally she spoke, but in a voice so low Heimrich could barely catch the words. He thought they were, "You're crazy," but he could not be entirely sure. Then she pulled herself forward to the edge of the chair.

"You're trying to make out that Jeff was jealous, aren't you?" she said, and now her voice rose and the words were no longer indistinct. "That's what you came here to ask about, isn't it? Not all this about Janet. You're—you're trying to drag Jeff into it, aren't you? All right, aren't you?"

"We don't drag people into things, Miss Selby," Heimrich said. His voice was very soft. "If they've dragged themselves into things we try to find out about it. That's all, Miss Selby.

"You're *awful*," she said. "Cruel and *awful*."

Then she leaned forward in the chair and put her hands over her face and began to cry.

"No," Heimrich said, and stood up. "Just a cop, Miss Selby."

She did not answer and did not look at him. She merely sat in the chair, her body shaking.

Merton Heimrich left her so.

13

There was no rush of business in the taproom of the Old Stone Inn when Heimrich went into it at a little after noon. There was, indeed, no business at all except for Lieutenant Charles Forniss, sitting at a corner table farthest from the bar. Tom, Dick or Harry—I've really got to find out what the man's name is, Heimrich thought—said, "I'll bring it right over, Inspector," to Heimrich's order of a martini, very dry. Heimrich went over to the corner table and sat down with Forniss.

"Frankel says he didn't see them start off that afternoon," Forniss said. "Says he went over and saddled up the horses and went back to planting glads. Says he didn't hear the Jeep start up. Rankin won't admit he wanted—wants now at a guess—to marry Miss Selby. But he did and does, I'm pretty sure. Does admit her mother broke up whatever was going on between them. Convinced Miss Selby it wouldn't be 'seemly.' Word he used, M.L. Not, he keeps on saying, that there was ever anything to break up."

Tom, Dick or Harry brought Merton Heimrich's martini. It had an olive in it. I've really got to learn this man's name, Heimrich thought, as he fished the olive out. He rather likes olives when they are not contaminating martinis, so he ate it.

"Yes," Heimrich said. "I got pretty much the same story from Dorothy Selby. Pretty much the same impression, too. And that Rankin didn't know she was going to marry Jameson until Jameson announced it. Too theatrically, she thinks. She's damned right on that. Lord of the manor most graciously agrees to marry an underling. Oh, he said all the right words. Just—left a feeling."

He sipped from his drink. The olive hadn't really damaged it too much. Of course the tang of the lemon peel oil was missing.

"Came as quite a jolt to Rankin, I'd think," Forniss said. "Assuming he didn't really know beforehand. Or—suspect beforehand, M.L.?"

Heimrich nodded his head slowly. He said, "Of course, he may have suspected, Charlie. And brought a bow and arrow along in the trunk of his car. A bit far-fetched. But possible, naturally. The nearest we've got to a motive, far's I can see. Wouldn't be the first time a man's knocked off a successful rival."

"Not by some thousands," Forniss said. "And Dr. Tennant may merely have lost his footing on those stairs and grabbed at the railing and—bango. And Mrs. Jameson's horse may have balked the jump and she went over his head into the wall. And Dorothy Selby may actually have told Rankin she was going to marry the old boy. And he may have picked up a bow and some arrows at the Selby house. They leave them lying around."

"She says he didn't even get out of his car when he stopped by to be guided to the Jameson party. Also, the arrows we saw there were wooden arrows, not steel."

"Yep," Forniss said, and finished his drink. He said, "You going to have another, M.L.?"

Heimrich shook his head. Forniss flicked a hand at Tom, Dick or Harry and pointed at his glass.

"Of course," Forniss said, "a steel arrow wouldn't be hard to get rid of. You could just stick it in the ground, I'd think."

"About Janet Jameson," Heimrich said, and regarded his almost-empty glass. He was, he realized, having second thoughts about it. The bartender came across the still-empty room carrying a tray with a glass on it, and ice in the glass, and a small pitcher of water and a jigger glass of bourbon. Heimrich let his second thought prevail and gestured toward his glass. He continued to look at his empty glass.

"About Janet Jameson?" Forniss said, and poured the contents of the jigger onto the ice in the squat glass and added a very little water.

"She may have ridden over the rise as Miss Jameson says she did," Heimrich said. "But then she may have rowed across and gone up the stairs to meet somebody. There may have been a quarrel and she may have got pushed down the stairs. Whoever pushed her may have rowed her body back across and lugged it down to the stone fence and arranged it for Miss Jameson to find."

"Yep," Forniss said. "We both thought of that, didn't we? And there'd have been time enough. And she didn't weigh very much."

Heimrich looked at him and said, "No, Charlie?"

"Both the Frankels say she was little," Forniss said. "Mrs. Frankel says she couldn't have weighed over a hundred pounds." He drank from his glass. He said, "This Ronald Jameson. The old man's son. He's a pretty husky guy, M.L."

Heimrich agreed that Ronald Jameson was a pretty husky guy. "Jameson was fond of his father's wife," Heimrich said. "Far as he'll go, naturally."

"And got damn annoyed when you asked him about it," Forniss said. "You think it was Jameson she went up the stairs to meet? And that he pushed her down them? Not what you'd do to somebody you were fond of, I wouldn't think. Still—"

"Yes, Charlie," Heimrich said. "People do quarrel. Get angry and do things they don't really mean to do."

"What we'd come up with," Forniss said, "is two violent deaths with nothing to tie them together. Except happening at the same place. This place they call The Tor."

"Not tidy, no," Heimrich said, and thought how unlikely words tend to get stuck in the mind. "Too bad, in a way, that young Jameson doesn't get a lot of money from his father's estate. Make things simpler, that way."

"Maybe he didn't know about his father's will," Forniss said. "Maybe he thought he'd get the lot. If his father didn't marry Miss Selby. That would have made a difference. Anyway, he could have thought it would."

Heimrich said, "Yes, Charlie," but not as if he had been listening very closely.

Forniss heard the inattention in the inspector's voice. He said, "All right. All we've got is theories."

Heimrich said, "Yes," again. Then he said, "They keep that fireplace going a lot in the living room, don't they? Or drawing room, whatever Miss Jameson calls it.

She likes warm rooms, of course. Probably her brother did, too."

Forniss used a forefinger to swish ice cubes in his glass. When Heimrich did not continue, he said, "Yeah, M.L.?"

"Oh," Heimrich said, "a handy place to burn a wooden bow, is all. It had turned chilly Sunday morning. Could be Barnes had a fire going early, before the family got down."

"Or fires," Forniss said. "There's a fireplace in the dining room too. One in the old boy's office, which doesn't look as if it's been used much lately. One in Miss Jameson's dressing room, too. Built before the day of central heating, the house was. Forced hot air now. Must have cost Jameson plenty to have it put in. Place like that. Built the way it probably is."

"We'd better ask Barnes about the fires Sunday morning," Heimrich said. "And whether he laid them the night before, when the wind shifted. There are sporting goods stores in Peekskill, aren't there?"

"A couple, anyway. And God knows how many in the city. Yes, we'd better. Get the local boys on it? You think somebody bought a bow, and a handful of steel arrows maybe, specially for the occasion?"

"The bow we found was about ready to fall apart," Heimrich said. "I shouldn't think a handful of arrows, Charlie. Two, in case the first one missed, probably. Perhaps only the one, if the shooter was pretty confident and had the range set in his mind. Short range from the pier to a man in the boat. Suppose—"

He stopped. The bartender was coming down the room with a tray with a cocktail glass on it in one hand and menu cards in the other. He put the glass down in front of Heimrich. There was an olive in the martini.

He said, "Like to order, gentlemen? Not that there's any—"

The telephone at the bar rang.

"Be right back," the bartender said, and went back up the room.

The telephone stopped ringing.

"We go up and ask Barnes about the fires yesterday morning," Heimrich said. "And give the locals a—"

The bartender interrupted him, calling down the length of the taproom. He said, "For you, Inspector," and held the telephone receiver up and waggled it in the air. Heimrich walked up the long room and spoke his name into the receiver.

"Farmer, T. J., Inspector. At the hospital up here. In—"

"Yes, Tom," Heimrich said to Detective Sergeant Thomas James Farmer, assigned to Troop K headquarters in Washington Hollow. "I know where you are. Got something?"

"Not much. Thing is, Dr. Tennant's begun to make sounds. Just that, so far. But the nurse has called the resident. She thinks maybe the patient is beginning to come out of it."

"Sounds, Tom?"

"All I could make out of it, sir. Just—oh, noises. But it was as if he was trying to say something. Not saying anything now. Yes, Doctor. Sure I will. Just one—"

There was a pause. There was a voice in the background.

"Sure," Farmer said, not into the telephone. "Doctor's just come in, Inspector. Wants the phone."

"Give it to him," Heimrich said. "And stay there. If they make a fuss, stay there anyway. Tell them I'll be along."

Sergeant Farmer said, "Sir," and hung up.

Heimrich went back to the corner table. He did not, however, sit at it. He took up his cocktail glass and drank the martini. He did not even bother to remove the olive.

"Tennant seems to be coming out of it," Heimrich said. "I'm going up to the hospital. You'll—"

"See Barnes," Forniss said. "Get them started on places that might sell bows and arrows. Yep, M.L."

"And," Heimrich said, "get yourself something to eat, huh?"

Forniss said, "Sir," like the Marine Corps officer he once had been. Heimrich laughed briefly and went out to the Buick. It took him only about twenty minutes to reach the Cold Harbor Memorial Hospital. It took him only another ten minutes to find a place to park the Buick. The place he found was in an area marked, "Physicians and Staff Only."

Dr. James Tennant's hospital room was large—large enough, Heimrich realized, for two beds. There was only one bed in it, and a nurse and the surgical resident Heimrich had met before were standing on either side of it, the doctor leaning down over Tennant.

Sergeant Farmer was sitting on a chair a little way from the bed. The physician turned when Heimrich went into the room and said, "Doctor—oh, it's you again."

"Yes," Heimrich said. "He's coming out of it, you think?"

"Could be," the surgeon said. "Thought you were Dr. Wenning. He's on his way up. Look, the patient's in no condition—"

"I know," Heimrich said. "I'll just take the sergeant's place for a while, Doctor."

He looked at Farmer, who shook his head and shrugged his shoulders and stood up. He said, "The barracks, Inspector?"

"No. Get yourself something to eat and stick around."

Farmer said, "Sir," as sergeant to inspector and went out of the room. Heimrich sat down in the chair Farmer had got up from. And the man in the hospital bed moaned. It was a low, broken moan.

"You're coming along fine, Doctor," the surgeon said to the man in the bed. "Just fine. Dr. Wenning will be along any minute."

He walked to the door. Heimrich went after him and outside the door the physician stopped. Heimrich said, "Is he, Doctor? Coming along fine?"

"Better than I expected," the doctor said. "Anyway, I think he heard me. Just before you got here I'd told him that Dr. Wenning was on his way up and he said, 'Frank?' Anyway, I think that was what he said. Wenning's first name is Frank."

"That's all he's said?"

"Nurse Latham thought he was trying to talk," the surgeon said. "Called me. I was just washing up, actually. Some girl smashed her car up and got thrown out. Wasn't much hurt apparently and was sitting in the emergency ward waiting until somebody could get to her and—keeled over. Turns out her tail is full of glass and she—well, I guess she thought it wouldn't be proper to mention it. Jesus!"

"Yes," Merton Heimrich said.

"I oughtn't to let you stay in there," the doctor said. "When Wenning shows up he'll probably get you thrown out."

"I won't disturb the patient," Heimrich said. "All I'll do is listen, Doctor."

The physician went off down an aseptic corridor, presumably to extract broken glass from the buttocks of a modest young woman. Heimrich went back into the hospital room and closed the door after him and went

200

to the chair Farmer had been sitting on and listened. All he heard was stertorous breathing from the bed and soft humming from Nurse Latham. He thought he might as well have had a sandwich, at least, before he came to the hospital. He thought, I didn't know they came that modest any more. No wonder the poor kid keeled over.

He waited for more than half an hour. Nurse Latham kept on humming, rather cheerfully under the circumstances, Heimrich thought. The man on the bed, his head only a white ball of bandages, kept on breathing, loudly at first and then more quietly. The door opened, and a tall stringy man in a white jacket which did not fit very well came into the room. He looked at Heimrich and said, "Who are you? What are you doing here?"

Heimrich said who he was and that he was listening.

"Hearing anything? I'm Dr. Wenning."

"Just his breathing," Heimrich said. "Seems he spoke your name, or tried to. Before I got here, that was."

Dr. Wenning said, "Mmmm," and went over to the bed and bent down over the bandaged head. He pushed back the eyelids and looked into the eyes. He took the chart off the foot of the bed and looked at it and again said, "Mmmm." He said, "Pressure hasn't come up much, has it, nurse? Beat's regular?"

"No, Doctor. Yes, it's regular. Soft, though."

"We'll stop the sedation for a while," Wenning said. "More just sleep now than coma, I'd say, wouldn't you, nurse?"

"Yes, Doctor."

The doctor nodded his head and, without turning toward Heimrich, said, "What are you listening for, Inspector?"

"Anything he says," Heimrich said. "You think he'll say anything, Doctor?"

"Eventually," Dr. Wenning said. "Not as much damage as I was afraid there'd be. Jim just fell downstairs, didn't he? Landed on his head?"

"He was found at the foot of a steep flight of stairs," Heimrich said. "Brick stairs. We assume he fell down them."

"So a police inspector sits in?"

"There's a railing down the stairs," Heimrich said. "One section of it pulled loose."

"All the same," Wenning said. "Still a bit unsteady on his legs, you know. Could account for it. Or would that be too simple?"

"A man was killed at the Jameson house yesterday morning," Heimrich said. "Not from falling downstairs. Mind telling me why you said 'still,' Doctor."

"Since the operation," Wenning said. "Abdominal aortic aneurysm. Didn't you know about that?"

Heimrich shook his head. He said, "That being, Doctor?"

"Permanent dilation of the aorta," Wenning said, and walked over and stood looking down at Inspector Heimrich. "Which is the main artery of the human body. His occurred in the abdomen. Corrected by vascular surgery. Benson. One of the best men in the field. Getting along all right, Jim is. From what I hear, anyway."

"Unsteady on his legs, Doctor?"

"An aneurysm reduces the flow of blood to the legs," Wenning said, his voice full of patience for ignorance. "They graft in tubing to replace the damaged artery. Normal blood sufficiency comes back. Not all at once, of course. He"—he gestured toward the bed—"had corrective surgery about six months ago. Recovering all right. Supposed to walk a bit—quite a bit—after that kind of surgery. If I know Jim, he's been taking his doctor's advice. Slow process, all the same."

202

"Be obvious when you saw him walking, this unsteadiness?"

"If you were looking for it," Wenning said. "He isn't a cripple or anything like that. Just, as I said, a little unsteady. A little—call it unsure. Tries to hide it, being the kind of man he is. Does most of the time, probably."

"Get off balance now and then?"

"Possibly. And have pains in his legs now and then. Drag a person down, an operation like that. On the table four or five hours, from what Benson tells me. A bit more extensive than the X rays indicated, at a guess. Not my line of country, Inspector."

Heimrich said he realized that.

"Speaking of your line of country," Heimrich said. "What's your prognosis about the head wound, Doctor?"

"Oh, optimistic, Inspector. No real brain damage to speak of. Some bone fragmentation. May have to put a plate in. We'll know more later."

"Damage to his mind?"

"I hope not. I think not. Damn good mind, Jim's got."

"He'll remember about the accident? About what happened just before it?"

Dr. Wenning shrugged his thin shoulders. He said, "You think we're fortunetellers, Inspector? Maybe. Maybe not."

"Any idea when he'll be able to talk?"

Again, Dr. Frank Wenning shrugged his shoulders.

"He's asleep now. When he wakes up, he may try to get out a few words. Perhaps this afternoon. More likely, in a week or so. And, I won't have him questioned. You understand that, Inspector?"

"Yes. I won't disturb your patient, Doctor. I'll just wait a—"

There were sounds from the man on the bed. At first

they were merely broken, tortured sounds. Then, almost clearly, the sounds turned to words.

Wenning was beside the bed by then, leaning over James Tennant. Heimrich stood up and moved a little closer to the bed.

"Eating into your," Tennant said, almost clearly.

Wenning spoke, his voice very low and soft. He said, "You know where you are, Jim?"

"Hos—" Tennant said, or something that sounded like it. Then, again, he began to breathe heavily. His breathing, Heimrich thought, was not as labored as it had been before.

Wenning went around the bed to the telephone on the other side of it. He said, "X-ray."

The telephone clicked and rasped at him. Then, less raspingly, words came through. "X-ray laboratory."

"Dr. Wenning. I want skull X rays of Dr. Tennant. Now."

He hung up. He said, "You heard me, Inspector."

"I heard you. You think he's coming out of it, Doctor?"

"Could be," Wenning said. "It just could be. The pressure may have let up a little. The pictures may show something. We'll—"

Dr. Frank Wenning's "now" evidently meant "now" to the X-ray lab. There was a knock on the door, and the door opened and two men in white uniforms wheeled a stretcher into the room.

Heimrich went out of the room. Sergeant Farmer sat on a chair just outside the room. He stood up when Heimrich came out.

"They're taking him to X-ray," Heimrich said. "When they bring him back, take over inside. And listen."

Farmer said, "Sir," and remained standing while

Heimrich walked down the corridor in the direction, he hoped, of elevators. He found an elevator and it stopped when he pressed a button. He got into it and pressed another button, this one numbered "3." He walked an aseptic corridor, a little slippery underfoot, to Room 323.

The door was partly open. Estelle Tennant was fully dressed. She was sitting in a chair and smoking a cigarette. Her young, pretty face was drawn. She looked at Heimrich as he went into the room and fear widened her eyes.

"He's doing all right," Heimrich said. "Dr. Wenning seems optimistic. He tried to talk, Mrs. Tennant. Even said a few words. Or almost said them."

"What words, Inspector?"

"Oh," Heimrich said, "nothing that seemed to mean much. 'Eating into your' was what it sounded like. Mean anything to you, Mrs. Tennant?"

She shook her head. Then she said, "That pain was eating into him?"

"Something like that, possibly," Heimrich said. He drew a light chair up and sat facing her.

"Dr. Wenning said something about your husband's having had an operation a while back," Heimrich said.

"Six months ago. He's been—he was getting along remarkably well, Dr. Benson told him. Making a really surprising recovery. We could both see that, too. We could all see that."

"Still a little unsure on his feet, Dr. Wenning thinks he may be. You've noticed that, Mrs. Tennant?"

"For a while," she said. "Almost not at all the last month or so." She put her cigarette out in the ashtray beside her. Then she said, "Oh—"

Heimrich waited.

"You think it was that?" she said. "That his legs

were—were not as strong as they had been. That that's why he fell?"

"It may have been, naturally," Heimrich said. "You say you could all see how much your husband was improving. You mean everybody who knew him, I suppose. Including everybody in your family. Your father. Your aunt. Your brother."

"Of course," she said. "We were all worried there for a time. It was—was such a long operation. Such a major operation. But he came through it wonderfully, Dr. Benson said. He's a strong man, really. A very strong man." She leaned forward in her chair and her voice rose a little. "He'll come through this," Estelle Tennant said.

"I'm sure he will," Heimrich said. "Dr. Wenning is sure he will. And, being a doctor, your husband will follow the advice his doctor gives him. Some people don't, I'm afraid."

"Of course he will," Estelle Tennant said.

"As he has been doing about walking, I gather," Heimrich said. "At Dr. Benson's advice, according to Dr. Wenning. To help restore the circulation in his legs."

She said, "Oh, yes. Every day. Faithfully every day. In the city he managed to get walks in between patients. But hadn't I already told you that?"

"Yes," Heimrich said. "I remember now, Mrs. Tennant."

"In town," she said, "over from the office—it's our house too, really—to Madison. Down Madison a block and along Central Park South to Columbus Circle and back to the house again. It's in Sixtieth Street, about halfway between Park and Madison. About twenty minutes, it always takes him."

Heimrich nodded his head. "People who walk for exercise," he said, "usually fall into patterns. Walk the same way each time, I mean. He took his regular walks up here too, I suppose. When you happened to be visiting your father and aunt."

"Yes. Oh, yes. Almost always the same way. Down—down those awful stairs to the lake. Then along the path by the lake and up the back way by the garden Aunt Ursula's so proud of. And up to the house."

"Taking the same time for it every day?"

"Within a minute or two. That's—that's why I got to worrying yesterday—was it only yesterday?—when he didn't come up to the room when I expected him to. And—and went to look for him."

"Yes," Heimrich said. "You knew the way he usually went, so you looked down the stairs."

She said, "Yes," and her voice shook. She said, "Do you have to make me remember, Inspector? Do you have to?"

"I'm sorry," Heimrich said. "I have to try to find out about things, you know. You went down from your room and over to the head of the staircase. That's the way it was?"

"I looked down toward the garden first, I think. To see if he—if he was coming. I didn't see him, so I went around and looked—looked down those dreadful stairs. And—and—" She moved her head slowly from side to side.

"I know," Heimrich said. "Have you and your husband been spending much time at your father's place, Mrs. Tennant? Since Dr. Tennant's operation?"

"A good deal of last month," she said. "August's always vacation time for him. A good many doctors take August off, you know. Specialists, I mean. Men like Jim."

"And while he was at The Tor, your husband took these daily walks of his? Down the stairs and around by the path and up that way usually?"

"Almost every day," she said. "Oh, if it was bad weather, he walked inside the house. Back and forth. Back and forth."

"At a certain time each day, Mrs. Tennant?"

"After lunch," she said. "Almost always after lunch."

"Did you ever go with him?"

"Down those stairs? Since I was—oh, quite a little girl—I've been afraid of those stairs. So steep. And—and you can see such a long way down. They've always frightened me."

"Scared me too, a little," Heimrich said. "The others at the house? Your father and aunt? Your brother?"

"Dad did," she said. "I don't really know about the others. Oh, Aunt Ursula doesn't ever, I think. She feels as I do about them. I don't know about Ron. I don't think he goes down to the lake much."

"Miss Selby use the stairs, do you happen to know?"

"I don't think so. Mostly she just came into the house and went through the living room to Dad's office. We don't—didn't—really see much of her. Except Dad, of course. Inspector—is Dr. Wenning really—does he really think Jim's going to be all right?"

"Yes, Mrs. Tennant. That's what he tells me."

"He wouldn't lie to you, would he? He might lie to me—try to make things easy for me. But there's no reason he should lie to you, is there?"

"No," Heimrich said. "I'm quite sure he was telling me what he really thinks, Mrs. Tennant. That your husband's going to be all right."

He stood up.

"Are you going to stay here for a while, Mrs. Tennant?" he asked her.

"Yes," she said. "I want to be near him. And—and I can't go back home just now. Back to The Tor, I mean. I—I've always loved it, but now it's turned bad for me."

"Yes," Heimrich said. "I'm sure your husband's going to be all right, Mrs. Tennant."

He found a telephone booth on the ground floor of the Cold Harbor Memorial Hospital.

Lieutenant Forniss had left the Old Stone Inn about an hour before. He had left word for the inspector that he was going to the Jameson house. He had also left word that he'd got the Peekskill police working on it and that the city police had agreed to do what they could, when they had the men to spare.

Heimrich drove north on NY 11F and up the winding drive to the big gray house on its hill. On its "tor," since Arthur Jameson had wanted it that way. Or his English ancestors had wanted it that way.

14

There was a pickup truck at the top of the drive, and Heimrich parked beside it. The words FERGUSON'S NURSERIES were lettered on the side of the truck. Under them were the words, "Shrubbery, Garden Maintenance, Small Pools a Specialty." From a short distance off, there was the clangor of metal on metal. Miss Ursula Jameson was finally getting the stair railing repaired. It was, Heimrich thought, rather late on for it. He went the other way, around the house and down toward the garden.

Frans Frankel was working in it. He had laid the excavated glads out in a neat row on the grass and in the sun. He was pulling up and throwing over the fence what Heimrich took to be frost-killed marigolds. He had his back to Heimrich and did not look around.

Heimrich found a downhill path and followed it. It was not too steep; did not plunge down like the steep brick staircase. It took him longer to reach the lake than it had by the stairs. The lake sparkled in the late

210

afternoon sun, and Heimrich walked a path beside it until he came to the foot of the staircase and the pier with the boat tied to it. He looked up the stairs, and it was a long way up. At the top, two men were wrenching lengths of iron pipe out of stanchions.

Merton Heimrich walked back the way he had come. The path toward the garden seemed steeper when you climbed it than when you went down. Frankel had finished with the marigolds. He was now pulling up what Heimrich took to have been zinnias.

Heimrich rang the doorbell of the gray stone house. It took Barnes a couple of minutes to answer it.

Yes, Lieutenant Forniss had been there. He had left word that, if the inspector showed up, he had gone back to the barracks. Yes, he had come in a police car with a trooper driving it. He had gone away in the same car.

Heimrich drove the Buick down the curving drive and north on NY 11F and northeast on US 44 to the Washington Hollow Barracks. He did not hurry; he thought that they had probably about finished for the day. He wondered whether James Tennant's mumbled words had been "eating into you" or whether there had been a final "r" on the word "you." To be followed by what? "Mind," perhaps? Dr. Tennant's specialty was the mind. As a neurologist the whole nervous system, of course. As a psychiatrist that infinitely complex tangle of nerves and cells in which the mind lives.

Heimrich parked the Buick in the space reserved for it; in the space with "Inspector Heimrich" painted on the pavement. Three spaces away was an outlined slot marked "Lt. Forniss." That space was empty. When he went past it, Forniss's small office also was empty.

Heimrich went on to his own office, which, as at Hawthorne, was a corner one with windows on two sides. Sunlight slanted into one of the windows. They'd put the heat on for the first time that fall. Heimrich turned it off and opened one of the windows a few inches. The air which came in was chilly air. He lifted his telephone and asked that Lieutenant Forniss be sent in when he returned—from wherever he was—and got an obedient "Sir."

His In basket was loaded; nowadays it was always loaded. A policeman never has only one thing to do at a time. Heimrich unloaded the In basket and began to go over the papers. He went over them with half a mind, which was all most of them deserved. He put his initials on where they were required. He made a telephone call and assured the Office of the District Attorney, County of Putnam, in Carmel that, no, he hadn't forgotten he was due in court Wednesday morning. He wondered where Charlie Forniss had got to. He thought that if Charlie didn't show up pretty soon he might as well go along to Van Brunt, leaving word that Charlie could reach him there.

Forniss came in a little before five. He sat on the opposite side of Heimrich's desk and put a thin cylinder of brown paper on the desk.

"Went over to Peekskill," Forniss said. "Happened to remember a man I know works in a sporting goods store there. After I'd been to the Jameson house."

Heimrich said, "Yes, Charlie?"

"They didn't have fire in the living room or the dining room Saturday night," Forniss said. "Warm night and too many people. Had big ornamental screens in front of both those fireplaces, because Miss Jameson doesn't like empty fireplaces. Says they make a room look unfinished."

"Yes," Heimrich said. "Even in summer we keep a fire laid in ours. The office fireplace?"

"Fire laid there," Forniss said. "Ready to be lighted.

Fireplace doesn't look as if it had been used much. Same in Jameson's room upstairs. Rooms, actually—bedroom and what looks like a sort of den-dressing room. Fire ready to be lighted. Looks as if it could have been laid all summer. We'd been over the room. Been over all the rooms. Left them as near as we could the way they were."

"Miss Jameson didn't object to your going over the house again?"

"She wasn't there, M.L. Gone into Cold Harbor, according to Barnes. She and her nephew. To look at coffins."

"It's something survivors have to do," Heimrich said. "Go ahead, Charlie."

"The wind shifted around two Sunday morning," Forniss said. "Cold northwest wind started up. Barnes laid fires in the living room and the dining room. Miss Jameson likes the house nice and warm, way he put it."

"And in Miss Jameson's dressing room? Sitting room or whatever she calls it?"

"He'd laid that earlier, he says. While the party was still going on. Carried logs and stuff up the back stairs and got the fire laid so she could light it if it was cold in the morning."

"As it turned out to be," Heimrich said. "Foresighted guy, Barnes."

"She did light it, M.L. Just ashes in the fireplace. Barnes doesn't know when. Says that, what with one thing and another, he's got behind on things a little."

"One thing being murder," Heimrich said. "The ashes were cold when you had a look at her fireplace today?"

"Yep. They use heavy wood, and coals would last quite a while. Cold and dead when the trooper and I had a look. And pawed around some in the ashes."

Heimrich nodded his head and waited.

Forniss unrolled the cylinder of brown paper. He took two objects out of it. One was a short sliver of blackened metal. The other object was charred and almost shapeless; burned out of whatever shape it once had had.

"Thing is," Forniss said, "this smells a little like leather. Burned leather. Half-burned leather."

He reached the shapeless object across the desk. Heimrich sniffed it. It smelled, he thought, like burned leather. It smelled of ashes.

"The man I know in Peekskill," Forniss said, "says he doesn't know much about bows. Not much demand for them. They do carry a few. Haven't sold any recently, far's he knows. Golf clubs and tennis rackets, yes. Two bows in stock and a few arrows. No steel arrows. We had a look at the bows."

"And, Charlie?"

"What he called 'backed bows,'" Forniss said. "Reinforced on the belly side. Side that's convex when you pull on the bow, I gather. The two they had in stock were backed with rawhide. Sometimes, he says, they use a tough wood, like hickory, for backing. And sometimes, M.L., they use a thin strip of steel."

He slid the sliver of metal he had taken from the wrapping across the desk toward Heimrich. Heimrich looked at it and then he looked at Forniss.

"Yes," Forniss said, "he thinks it could be, M.L. About the right length and right thickness, he thinks. Says he can't be sure because he really doesn't know much about bows. Just says it looks about the right size. It does to me, too, M.L."

Heimrich looked again at the sliver of metal.

"Yes," he said, "it does to me, Charlie. This—this wad of what's maybe half-burned leather—your friend have any theories about it, Charlie?"

214

"Most bows," Forniss said, "apparently have a grip where you hold on to them. Sometimes just taping, he thinks. Sometimes a sort of plush. And sometimes leather. Barnes just took up enough wood for one fire, he says. So it couldn't have been kept going. Leather doesn't burn like wood, M.L."

"No," Heimrich said. "Miss Jameson says she didn't know anything about her brother until a maid waked her up. Presumably she was alone in this suite of hers. From the layout, Charlie, do you think anybody could have sneaked in and lighted her fire? Adding a bow to it? I mean, is there a door between the two rooms?"

"No," Forniss said. "Just a sort of archway. And the door into the suite squeaks a little when you open it. She'd have to be a—"

The telephone rang on Heimrich's desk. He reached for it and, at the same time, finished Forniss's sentence. "Pretty heavy sleeper," Heimrich said to Forniss and, to the telephone, "Heimrich." Then he said, "Yes, Sergeant?"

"Nothing that means very much, far's I can see," Sergeant T. J. Farmer said. "But you said you wanted everything. He said a few words again. The 'eating into your' again."

"You, Sergeant? Or, 'your'?"

"Your, way I got it."

"As if he were speaking to somebody else? Or remembering what he'd said to somebody else?"

"Sort of sounded that way to me, Inspector."

"That was all you could make out?"

"One other thing, Inspector. Pretty blurred. Sounded like 'conscious', or something like that. Maybe just trying to say he was conscious, I guess."

"Could it have been 'subconscious,' Sergeant?"

"Could have been almost anything," Farmer said. "Yes, I guess it could have been 'subconscious,' Inspector."

"All right," Heimrich said. "You in Dr. Tennant's room now, Sergeant?"

Farmer was not. The nurse had insisted that the telephone there be kept free. He had found a telephone down the corridor.

"Go back and keep listening," Heimrich said. "If Dr. Tennant says anything more—*anything*, Sergeant—call me—" He paused for an instant. "Call me at the Jameson house," he said.

He put the receiver back in its stand. Forniss was already half way up from the chair on the other side of Heimrich's desk.

"Yep, M.L.," Forniss said. He wrapped the steel sliver and what smelled like burned leather in the brown paper and put the parcel in a pocket. They went out of the office and along a corridor and down to the parking lot. They went down from the barracks onto NY 11F. Heimrich didn't push the Buick, but he kept it moving.

They were beyond Cold Harbor when Heimrich said, "These backstairs Barnes carried the wood up. Where's the bottom of them? In the kitchen?"

"Hallway off it."

"And the top?"

"End of the corridor Miss Jameson's suite opens on." Heimrich said, "Mmmm."

"This hallway at the foot of the stairs," Forniss said. "Got a door in it; door to outside. Opens on a stoop. There's a woodpile outside. Keep it covered with a tarp."

"Cement walk along the side of the house," Forniss said. "For delivery men, I suppose. And, going away from the house, going toward the garden, there's a path. Pine bark, looks to be."

216

Heimrich said, "Mmmm." He turned the Buick into the driveway of The Tor. "Probably," Heimrich said, "it connects with the path down to the lake. What Frankel calls 'the back way' to the lake."

"Yep," Forniss said.

The nursery truck was no longer parked in front of the big house, and from the brick staircase there was no longer the clanking of metal on metal. Repairs finished, or repairmen finished for the day. Geoffrey Rankin's big car was not parked in the turnaround. A State Police cruiser was, with a trooper in it. The radio chattered in the car, but not loudly. The trooper got out of the cruiser when the Buick stopped beside it.

"Mr. Rankin took off, Inspector," the trooper said. "Stopped and said he was driving into the village if you wanted to know and that I could save gas by not following him. Said he'd be back. Maybe I should have followed him just the same, sir?"

"No," Heimrich said. "You were right to save gas, Trooper."

Barnes opened the door at the first sound of the chimes. It was almost as if he had been expecting them. Yes, Miss Jameson and Mr. Jameson were at home. If they would—

The blaring of a telephone bell interrupted him.

"I'd better answer it," Barnes said. "Been ringing all day. Bothers Miss Jameson."

He went to the telephone at the back of the entrance hall. He said, "The Tor." he said, "Yes, he is. One moment, please," and turned and said, "It's for you, Inspector."

Heimrich walked the few steps and said, "Heimrich," into the telephone. He said, "Yes, Sergeant."

"You said 'everything,' sir," Sergeant Farmer said, "whether it meant anything or not. They've taken him somewhere for something they call a 'brain scan.' The nurse says it's something that shows clots. If there are clots."

"All right, Tom," Heimrich said. "You're still in the room? He's said something more?"

"Well," Farmer said, "almost, I guess. What I mean, words that are almost words."

Heimrich was patient. He said, "Almost what words, Tom?"   •

"Once something that sounded like 'fiddle.' To me, anyway. There was a kind of hissing sound and then what sounded like 'fiddle.' The nurse thought it sounded like that too, Inspector. Grace Burton, the nurse is, the one who's on now, I mean."

"Yes, Sergeant," Heimrich said. "Something that sounded like the word 'fiddle' with a sibilant sound before it. An 's' sound?"

"Way it sounded to me, sir. You did say everything he said. Whether it meant anything or not."

There was a defensive note in Sergeant Farmer's voice.

"Yes, Tom, everything," Heimrich said. "That's all he said?"

"Sounds," Farmer said, "as if he was trying to say something. All sort of garbled, the poor guy. Nothing I could be sure about. Once something like 'housekeeper,' the nurse thought. She was right by his bed. All I could hear was just sort of a sound."

" 'Fiddle,' " Heimrich said. "Something the nurse thought sounded like 'housekeeper.' Nothing else?"

"That's all I could get, sir. Whether it made any sense or not. That's what you meant, wasn't it, Inspector?"

"Yes," Heimrich said. "Just stay with it, Sergeant. I'll get you a relief by eight or so."

Farmer said, "Yes, sir." He also said, "Grace got me some coffee."

218

"That's good," Heimrich said and hung up. He said, "If you'll tell Miss Jameson I'd like to see her," to Barnes.

"Miss Jameson and Mr. Ronald are in the drawing room, sir. If you'll just—"

Heimrich and Forniss followed Barnes. When speech is difficult, sibilants come hardest, Merton Heimrich thought.

Ursula Jameson and her nephew were sitting side by side on the sofa in front of the fireplace. A contented fire was burning in the fireplace, and the two had drinks on the table in front of the sofa.

As Heimrich and Forniss walked down the room toward them, Jameson said, "Evening." It was a gruff greeting. Ursula Jameson did not say anything, but she looked at them. Then she nodded her head.

When the two big men reached the sofa, Ursula Jameson did speak. She said, "Something more, Inspector? Sit down, both of you. I'll have Barnes—"

"No," Heimrich said. "We don't want anything, Miss Jameson. Yes. One or two things more."

"Oh, what about poor Jim, Inspector? Jim Tennant? They won't tell us anything at the hospital. They don't even tell Estelle anything."

"The doctors are optimistic about Dr. Tennant," Heimrich said. "Expect him to recover fully, they tell me."

"He's still unconscious, isn't he? That's what they mean when they say he's resting comfortably, isn't it?"

"They think he's beginning to recover consciousness," Heimrich said. "At any rate—"

Ursula Jameson interrupted him. Her voice was quick. "You mean he's begun to talk?" she said. "Is that what you mean?" The question was abrupt.

Heimrich did not answer the abrupt question. He said, "Lieutenant, you might get that statement from Mr.

Jameson now. I'm sure Miss Jameson won't mind your using the typewriter in her brother's office."

Ursula Jameson merely looked fixedly at the fire.

Forniss said "Sir" as a Marine Corps captain acknowledges an order from a Marine Corps colonel. There was no uncertainty in the word. What was in Charles Forniss's mind was another matter.

"About the event of two years ago last May," Heimrich said.

Forniss said "Sir" again. He said, "Mr. Jameson—?"

The heavy-set black-haired man stood up, slowly. He said, "A lot of damn nonsense, for my money."

"We're supposed to get things written down," Heimrich told him. "They like things on paper, Mr. Jameson. Get the statement out of the way and you can get back to town as you've been wanting to. Shouldn't take more than ten or fifteen minutes, the statement shouldn't."

Jameson said, "O.K.," and went down the long room. Forniss went after him.

Ursula Jameson continued to look at the slow-burning fire. Heimrich said nothing until Jameson and Lieutenant Forniss had gone through the doorway at the end of the long room.

"Dr. Tennant has said a few words," Heimrich told the black-clad woman, who did not turn toward him, who looked only at the ebbing fire. "Tried to, anyway. Not much sense to them, I'm afraid. Unless you can help us, perhaps."

She said. "Words? What words? How could I possibly help?"

"Something that sounded like 'eating into,'" Heimrich told her. "May have been speaking of his own pain, of course. Although he's had shots to stop the pain. And something that sounded, to his nurse, like the word 'housekeeper.' Mean anything to you, Miss Jameson?"

She was listening. But she merely shook her head.

"And what sounded to the man we have in the room with Dr. Tennant like 'fiddle,'" Heimrich said. "Before that, a word which wasn't really a word, a sort of hissing sound, our man thought. As if he were trying to say a word with an 's' sound in it. As if—"

Ursula Jameson did not look away from the fire. She seemed to speak to the fire. The simple word she said was a mumble, was hardly more distinct than the words spoken by James Tennant had been. "I can't hear you, Miss Jameson," Heimrich said.

She did not turn from the fire, but she spoke again. The words were a little clearer.

" 'Second,' " Ursula Jameson said. "Second fiddle."

"Yes," Heimrich said. "I thought it might be. Remembering words he spoke to you, isn't he? Before he went out after lunch for his regular walk. Some hours before, I'd think. Because you'd have needed time. Not too much, probably. The rail came loose quite easily, I'd think. The rail he trusted to."

She looked at him then. Her dark eyes seemed very deep in her long, wrinkled face.

"I've no idea what you're talking about," Ursula said. The words were quite clear now. They were even a little loud.

"What Dr. Tennant said to you before his accident," Heimrich said. "After he told you why he thought you had killed your brother. When he was telling you, as a psychiatrist and a man who knew you well, what he thought had happened to your mind. What had been eating into it for years. Wasn't it that way, Miss Jameson?"

"Of course not," she said. "You must be—you must be insane, Inspector."

Heimrich shook his head slowly.

"No," Heimrich said. "Not I, Miss Jameson. You did

kill your brother, didn't you? Because you couldn't let
happen to you again what had happened so much of your
life. All of your life, almost. Playing second fiddle to
two women who—what, Miss Jameson? Usurped what
you felt was yours? What was all you really had. Isn't
that what Dr. Tennant told you? Before you tried to
kill him so he couldn't tell anybody else? Tell me, for
one. Arranged for him to fall down that staircase?
You'd done that before, hadn't you?"

She did not answer. She sat motionless, gazing into
the dwindling fire.

It was growing dusky in the room. The lights needed
turning on. The fire needed building up. Momentarily,
Heimrich thought of ringing for Barnes. But it was not
his house. The house belonged to the black-clad woman.
In the dimming light, her profiled face was like some
grotesque mask.

Merton Heimrich wanted to stand and leave the room;
wanted to get his mind out of the shadows creeping over
it. Inspector Heimrich could not leave the room. He had
to go on with it.

"He kept on bringing strangers in, didn't he?" Heimrich said. "New women, new wives, for you to keep
house for. Your house. The house you had lived all your
life in. Were you born here in The Tor, Miss Jameson?"

He waited a second for her to answer. She did not.

"He was going to bring another wife here," Heimrich
said. "To be—I suppose you thought of it as mistress
of your house. You killed him to stop that, didn't you?
Answer me, Miss Jameson."

She did not answer him.

"You killed his second wife, didn't you? Pushed her
down the stairs and went down after her to be sure she
was dead. Was she, Miss Jameson, or did you have to
finish the job?"

222

Again he waited for an answer. He waited without much hope. But the woman spoke from her grotesque mask—the ugly woman whose brother had twice brought beauty into the house and had planned once more to bring youth and beauty in.

"She was dead," Ursula Jameson told the fire. Heimrich could just hear the dead voice.

He waited for her to go on. She merely stared toward the fire. But it was not really a fire any more.

"Rowed her body across to the other side," Heimrich said. "Rowed back in the boat and got the Jeep and went around by the road. Got her body into the Jeep and took it down to the wall and arranged it there. Untethered the horses you'd had Frankel saddle. Left one near the wall and the other near the stable. And drove back in the Jeep to tell about this terrible accident. That's the way it was, wasn't it?"

She turned from the fire then and faced Heimrich.

"There is nothing you can prove, is there?" she said, and her voice was strong. It was high-pitched but it was strong.

"About Janet Jameson's death, no," Heimrich said.

"About any of this," she said. "You're just making it all up, aren't you? To frighten an old woman. This is my house, Inspector. Get out of it. Get out of my house."

She almost screamed the words at him.

Heimrich merely shook his head. He looked down the long room. Lieutenant Forniss was standing with his back to a closed door. Heimrich beckoned with his head, and Forniss walked up the room.

"The package, Charlie," Heimrich said, and Forniss gave him the cylinder of brown paper. Heimrich's fingers twisted it open.

"Miss Jameson," Heimrich said, "it was just between us before. Now Lieutenant Forniss is a witness. He will

223

take notes of what you say. You do not need to say anything without having a lawyer present. Because, Miss Jameson, I am going to arrest you on a charge of murder."

She only looked at him. He held the strip of steel and the shapeless wad of burned leather out toward her. She looked at them and then looked up at him.

"The steel backing of the bow you used," Heimrich said. "What's left of the leather grip. Didn't you know there was steel backing in your bow when you burned it in your fireplace? After you used it to kill your brother?"

She leaned toward the proof he was holding out for her to see.

"Steel?" she said, and her voice was muffled again. "Steel? But that was the arrow, wasn't it? The steel arrow. The steel—"

Then she fell sidewise on the sofa. Forniss caught her, or she would have fallen off it.

"Fainted," Heimrich said. "Better ring for Barnes. Have him get one of the maids to get her upstairs."

Forniss went to the dangling plush cord and pulled on it.

"And for God's sake," Heimrich said, "find a switch and let's get some light in this damn place."

Charles Forniss found a light switch.

15

Forniss moved Ursula Jameson so that she lay on the sofa and felt for her pulse. Heimrich went to the telephone. He called the Bureau of Criminal Investigation at the headquarters of Troop K in Washington Hollow and told the duty officer how things stood and what he wanted. He wanted Sergeant Farmer relieved at the hospital. He wanted troopers at The Tor. They were to report to Lieutenant Forniss. He called the hospital and got Farmer. Dr. Tennant was sleeping. He had not said, or tried to say, anything more. Farmer was told his relief was on the way. Farmer said, "Sir."

Heimrich put the telephone in its cabinet. Forniss had come up the room and was standing beside him. Heimrich said, "Yes, Charlie?"

"She doesn't seem to be coming out of it," Charles Forniss said. "And her pulse feels fluttery. Maybe—"

Barnes knew the name of the doctor. "Not that either of them needed a doctor very often." Dr. Jenkins answered his telephone. He listened. "Ursula's tough as nails," he said. "Of course she's been under a hell of a strain. Oh, all right, I suppose I'd better. Damn. About half an hour. Probably be O.K. by the time I get there, but all right."

"I'll leave it to you to tidy up," Heimrich told Charles Forniss.

Forniss said, "Sure, M.L."

"Because, between us, I want to get the hell out of here," Heimrich said. "Call me at home after the doctor's seen her."

"Sure, M.L."

There was chill dampness in the air Merton Heimrich stepped out into. The wind had died down and shifted. It blew flutters of fog from the hill top. It will rain tomorrow, Heimrich thought. This high up it may even start as snow. He got into the Buick and drove down the steep, winding drive. He drove south on NY 11F, his headlights gnawing holes in the darkness. When he was halfway home, rain showed up in the light beam and he set the wipers swishing.

Light streamed from the windows of the long, low house which once had been a barn. When the Buick was in the garage and he walked back to the door, the door was open. Susan stood in the doorway, with Colonel on one side and Mite on the other. They all looked up at him. Behind them flames leaped in the fireplace. The room was bright with light. Susan said, "Hi," and the word was bright. But then, looking up into his face, she said, "Are you all right, dear?"

"Now," Merton Heimrich said, and went into the bright room. He crossed to the fireplace and stood looking down at the fire. He turned and looked at Susan.

"His sister killed him," Heimrich said. "And I feel as

if I've been beating an old woman—a sick old woman. And I need—"

"Of course you do," Susan said and moved closer and took one of his hands in both of hers. She pressed his hand with hers and released it. She said, "I'll get them. Sit by the fire and I'll get them. You look so tired, darling."

"Not—" Heimrich said, but did not finish, because Susan had gone out of the room. He heard ice clattering in the mixer. She's stirring faster than usual, Merton Heimrich thought, and sat in one of the deep chairs in front of the fire. I've no real reason to feel tired.

Susan brought the shaker and glasses with frost on the bowls on a tray and put it down on the table between the two deep chairs in front of the fire. Susan sat in the chair on the other side of the small, round table. She poured from the shaker into the two chilled glasses. They clicked glasses and sipped from them.

"Better now?" Susan said, after they had sat for a moment looking first at each other and then at their fire.

"Much better now," Merton said. "Sometimes I almost—"

The jangle of the telephone interrupted him.

"I'll—" Susan Heimrich said, but Merton was already across the room. He said, "Yes, Charlie," into the phone and listened. He said, "I suppose it's the best thing. See you in the morning."

He went back to his chair and drank from his glass.

"Sometimes you almost what, dear?" Susan said.

"Hate my job," Heimrich said.

"Not really," Susan told him. "Not ever, really."

"No," Heimrich said, "Not really. Her doctor's sent Ursula Jameson out of her house. To the hospital.

There'll be a trooper in the corridor outside her door. When she wakes up she won't be in her house. She'll be in a strange place. She killed for the house, Susan. Killed twice and tried to kill again."

He sipped from his glass. Susan waited. Merton told her about Ursula Jameson.

"Because he was always taking her house away from her," Susan said. "Giving it to other women. And, of course, because she's very ugly. Has had to live all her life with ugliness. That would be hard on any woman, dear."

"Yes," Heimrich said, and looked across the table at his wife. She gets better-looking all the time, Merton Heimrich thought. How does she know what it would be like to be ugly?

"But not," Susan said, "hard to the point of killing about it. However long you've brooded. What will happen to her, Merton?"

"If I were her lawyer," Merton Heimrich said, "I'd try not guilty by reason of insanity. Since I'm not, I'll make us drinks."

He took the tray and mixer and empty glasses into the kitchen. There would be fresh glasses chilling in the freezer.

I don't hate my job, Merton Heimrich thought as he measured gin and vermouth onto ice. There are draining moments in any job, I suppose.

It's bright here and Susan's here. I'm not tired any more. I'm not in shadows any more.

He carried tray and a mixer and chilled glasses back to the brightness of the fire and the brightness which was around his wife.